Could this be how it happened to April?

Raven's eyes popped open. Was it her imagination, or were Vaughn's fingers tightening around her neck? *Had Vaughn planned this whole evening? Did he have something in mind other than romance?* She tried to push the ugly thoughts away, and then she tried to wrestle out of his grasp.

"Trying to get away already?" Vaughn asked playfully. He rolled Raven into a wrestling hold, leaving his powerful hand clasped around her throat.

Raven coughed. He wasn't letting go. She could feel his pulse racing through his fingers into the soft skin of her neck. It was terrifying, yet strangely exciting. *Could this be how it happened to April?* Raven struggled to break his hold, but it was useless. She was losing her breath now . . .

Find out Who Killed Peggy Sue?
Read:

Available from Puffin Books

Who Killed Peggy Sue?

If Looks Could Kill

Created by Eileen Goudge

PUFFIN BOOKS

PUFFIN BOOKS
Published by the Penguin Group
Viking Penguin, a division of Penguin Books USA Inc.,
375 Hudson Street, New York, New York 10014, U.S.A.
Penguin Books Ltd, 27 Wrights Lane, London W8 5TZ, England
Penguin Books Australia Ltd, Ringwood, Victoria, Australia
Penguin Books Canada Ltd, 2801 John Street, Markham, Ontario,
Canada L3R 1B4
Penguin Books (N.Z.) Ltd, 182–190 Wairau Road, Auckland 10, New Zealand

Penguin Books Ltd, Registered Offices: Harmondsworth, Middlesex, England

First published in 1991 by Viking Penguin, a division of Penguin Books USA Inc.

1 3 5 7 9 10 8 6 4 2

Produced by Daniel Weiss Associates, Inc.
33 West 17th Street, New York, New York 10011
Copyright © 1991 Eileen Zuckerman and Daniel Weiss Associates, Inc.
Cover illustration copyright © 1991 Daniel Weiss Associates, Inc.
All rights reserved

Library of Congress Catalog Card Number: 91-52873
ISBN 0-14-034889-1
Printed in the United States of America
Set in Avanta

CHAPTER 1

Raven let her hand trail through the dark water of the lake. She tried to empty her mind of all thought, and just feel the coolness of the evening and the breeze. She closed her eyes and listened to the gentle, rhythmic splash of oars as Vaughn rowed the small boat away from the shoreline of Hidden Valley.

It was a perfect night. The murder and all the awful things that had happened in its wake had been left behind, back in Paradiso. The sky and water met in a seamless black, velvet backdrop. On the horizon a sprinkling of stars and the narrow crescent of a moon shone as clear as ice.

"Feeling better?" Vaughn asked huskily. He stopped rowing and shifted over to sit next to Raven. He circled his arms around her as the rowboat drifted slowly on its own.

"Mmm," Raven whispered in his ear.

"I'm glad I finally got you to myself," Vaughn said. "Mr. Woolery may have scared the daylights out of you in the scrublands, but at least he gave me an excuse to take you away." Vaughn kissed her brow. "Just what I want. No one within miles but you and me. Just the two of us."

Just the two of us. Like April and her killer. Like Mr. Woolery and Raven only a few hours earlier. Raven felt a jolt of fear at the memories. "Do you think Mr. Woolery really might be the killer?" she asked.

"I don't know," Vaughn said, his voice warm against Raven's cheek. "Mr. Woolery always seemed like a pretty cool guy to me. Until now. But how well can you really know a teacher you see a couple of times a week for art class? Especially a new teacher."

Raven shrugged, feeling her shoulders move against Vaughn's chest as he held her, running his fingers through her long, jet black hair. "I guess the question is, how well do you really know most people when you get right down to it?" she said. "You read all those stories in the papers about people who are such good neighbors, good parents, good friends, and then they snap and commit unthinkable crimes."

Raven wondered if something like that had happened in Paradiso. Was April's murderer a respected citizen, someone's favorite teacher, best friend, or . . . boyfriend?

Raven pulled back from Vaughn's hug. The darkness, which just a few moments ago enveloped her in tranquility, felt frightening, unknowable. The lake was a well of blackness. The sky seemed to be closing in on her. She couldn't see anything past the prow of the little rowboat. She had the sudden, impossible urge to turn on some lights and see what was lurking around the edges of her perfect night.

"Hey, you okay?" Vaughn asked.

"I'm still a little creeped out, I guess," Raven answered. She realized she was shivering beneath her light cotton dress. "Or maybe I'm just getting cold."

"Want to go back to the cabin and I'll make us a fire?" Vaughn suggested.

"Sounds nice," Raven said. As Vaughn began to row again, the steady dip of the oars and the rocking of the little boat lulled her back to a feeling of relaxation.

Soon, Raven was bundled up in a soft quilt in front of the fire, and Vaughn added another log to the flames. The simple cabin had no electricity, so the only other light was from the two candles Vaughn had lit. Soft shadows flickered on the redwood beams and walls and then larger, wilder shadows as the fire caught, snapping and popping to life.

Vaughn replaced the gate over the fireplace and sat down close to Raven. She wrapped him in the quilt with her. "This is great," she whispered. "I feel like we've gone back in time here." She let her hand run up and down his back. "It's kind of funny that your family has this place. It feels more like one of the little huts in Mexico some of my relatives live in than, well—"

"Than big-business-Lars-Cutter's country palace?" Vaughn supplied. He laughed. "It reminds Dad of the cabin in the New Hampshire mountains where he used to go with his parents. It's his New England nostalgia or something. Every once in a while he pretends he's a Pilgrim. Just to see where it all started." Vaughn searched for Raven's hand under the quilt and entwined his fingers with hers. "Whatever it is, I'm glad we have this place."

"Good for your love life, huh?" Raven whispered, breathing in the pungent, smoky smell of the fire, mixed with the scent of Vaughn's cologne and the crisp freshness of the country night.

Vaughn brushed her forehead with his lips. "Well, I've gotta admit I've been dreaming about getting you up here ever since I asked you to the Peach Blossom Ball."

Raven smiled, thinking about the first time Vaughn had mentioned the Peach Blossom Festival Ball. It was at a meeting of the organization Raven headed, SCAM, Students Concerned About the Mall. Raven was fighting what seemed to be a losing battle to save the Paradiso scrublands from being paved over and destroyed forever.

The mall was the pet project of Lacey Pinkerton's dad, Calvin Pinkerton—the richest, most influential man in Paradiso. Unfortunately, Vaughn's dad, Lars Cutter, was Cal Pinkerton's partner. It had taken Vaughn a while to get up enough guts to speak out against his father. But when he'd finally shown up at a SCAM meeting, Raven had grabbed the opportunity to get to know him better. She'd secretly had her eye on him even before he and Lacey had broken up. Although it had been pouring outside during the meeting, Raven remembered thinking that Vaughn's eyes were as blue as the sky on a sunny day.

She turned her face up toward his and their lips met. They kissed softly. Then more passionately. "That meeting seems like such a long time ago," Raven whispered. It had been only a few weeks, but the fact that it was before April Lovewell's murder made it feel as if it had happened in another lifetime.

"I'm still looking forward to dancing with you at the ball," Vaughn murmured between kisses. "Pretty Peggy Sue."

Raven laughed. Peggy Sue was what the kids at school had nicknamed the Queen of the Peach Blossom Festival in honor of this year's 1950s theme. "Vaughn, they haven't even rescheduled the festival yet." April's murder had put the town's biggest annual event on hold. "Besides, I've got some pretty stiff competition for Queen. And now Kiki's work on the April Lovewell Memorial Foundation is sure to get her plenty of support from the selection committee. Besides, Kiki's really great. I mean, I'll bet you'd vote for her if I wasn't in the contest, right?"

"Well, yeah, but Kiki and I grew up together on the Hill. She's one of my oldest friends."

"Exactly. And there's a good reason. That's my point," Raven said. "And Lacey . . . well, she might not be my choice, but she *is* the most popular girl at school."

"Her," Vaughn said flatly.

"Lots of people think she walks on water." Raven gave Vaughn a teasing poke in the ribs. "Come on, Vaughn. You of all people know Lacey Pinkerton's pretty hot."

Vaughn put on his best scowl. "Okay, the girl's good looking. I won't deny that. And she can be a lot of fun when she feels like it. But then you get a glimpse of her riding around on her broomstick, and you know what she's really like."

"Well, maybe you and I think that, but plenty of people disagree. Face it. The whole school's in love with her. She's got the best chance to win of the three of us."

"I don't know," said Vaughn. "That's what people were saying last time, too. And then April won."

"And look where it got her," Raven said. She shuddered, suddenly feeling isolated way out there by the lake. She glanced out the window behind her, half anticipating a face peering in at them. But the pane was black to the night. She turned back to Vaughn. *Just the two of us . . .* she thought nervously. And then, Get a hold of yourself, Raven, she scolded herself.

"Maybe I shouldn't have brought up the Peach Blossom Festival in the first place," Vaughn said, "but I can't wait to see you become Queen. Besides, I know how much you want the scholarship that goes with the crown."

Raven nodded. It was her reason for being in the contest at all. She'd gotten into a number of good colleges, but Stanford, her first choice, hadn't come up with enough financial aid for her to accept their offer. Yet.

Raven knew Lacey was in the contest for the glory and glamour, and the Hollywood screen test that was the other prize. But for Raven, being Peach Blossom Queen was her ticket out of Paradiso. She wanted it badly. And she deserved it. But she didn't want to get her hopes up.

"Vaughn, let's not think about what's going to happen. Or what's happened," she said. "Okay? Let's not think about anything at all."

"I like that idea," Vaughn said. They were quiet for

7

a few minutes, listening to the flames lick at the logs in the fireplace. Raven concentrated on Vaughn's nearness as her eyes followed the dancing shadows cast by the fire. One of them kept lapping at the edge of a plate-size hole in the wood wall by the foot of the cabin door.

"What happened there?" Raven asked, pointing.

Vaughn's gaze followed her finger. His frown carved deep lines on his handsome, square-jawed face. "Nothing much."

"What do you mean, nothing much?" Raven asked.

The frown stayed on Vaughn's face. "Raven," he said, "I know you want to be a great lawyer and everything, but I'm not on the witness stand."

Raven let go of his hand. "Whoa! Okay, okay. I wasn't accusing you of anything. I was just asking."

Vaughn let out a long breath. "Look, I'm sorry. I—I got mad at someone, all right? I sort of lost it and kicked the wall."

"You were so mad at somebody you put a hole that size through a solid wall? Who could get you so mad? Your dad?" Raven knew Vaughn was having plenty of problems with his parents over his involvement with SCAM.

"My dad? Nah, we're past the fighting stage."

"Who, then?"

Vaughn shook his head. "I thought you didn't want to think about anything, Raven."

"You got me curious," Raven said. That and a little nervous. She knew Vaughn had a temper—she'd seen it in school a few times when someone had gotten him especially riled up, and she'd seen it when he competed in his wrestling matches. But to see signs of it here, in this peaceful, out-of-the-way cabin, was scary. *Just the two of us.* "Who, Vaughn?"

Vaughn worked his jaw. Then he said, "Lacey. I was up here with Lacey and we had a really big fight."

"Oh." Well, you asked, Raven told herself. She felt a sizzle of jealousy at the idea of Lacey and Vaughn together up here, maybe right in front of the fire like she and Vaughn were now. She looked at the hole. Things obviously hadn't turned out the way Lacey and Vaughn had expected.

She could definitely understand getting furious at Lacey Pinkerton. Like father, like daughter. Calvin Pinkerton had tried to bribe Raven out of fighting the mall by offering to pay her college tuition. He was so smug and condescending, sauntering into Rosa's Café with Darla, Lacey's mother, the queen of nasty in her dark sunglasses. He'd slipped Raven a one-hundred-dollar bill as she waited on tables. Then he'd hinted about the bigger payoffs to come.

But forget it, Raven. Just forget it, she told herself. You're here to get away from the trouble in Paradiso

—for tonight, at least. She took Vaughn's hand again, bringing it to her lips. Then she turned her face toward his. He was so handsome. She felt her pulse take off as she studied his chiseled features and looked into his clear, clear blue eyes.

"Vaughn, kiss me," she said softly.

Vaughn didn't answer. He leaned toward her and their lips touched. The fire crackled. Raven shivered. Vaughn drew her into an embrace, and they fell back on the braided rug in front of the fireplace. Raven could feel their hearts beating against each other. He held her face in his hands and kissed every part of it. Her hands traced the ripple of muscles up his arms and down his chest. Their mouths met again. Their kisses grew deeper, more probing. Raven felt a sigh rise in her throat.

Later, she lay in his arms by the dying embers of the fire. "Vaughn, I wish we never had to go back," she said sleepily.

"Mm," Vaughn murmured. He stroked her face, then her throat. He let his fingers rest softly there. "That could be arranged."

Raven's eyes popped open. Was it her imagination, or were Vaughn's fingers tightening around her neck? Had Vaughn planned this whole evening? Did he have something in mind other than romance? She tried to push the ugly thoughts away, and then she tried to wrestle out of his grasp.

"Trying to get away already?" Vaughn asked playfully. He rolled Raven into a wrestling hold, the whole time leaving his powerful hand clasped around her throat.

Raven coughed. He wasn't letting go. She could feel his pulse racing through his fingers into the soft skin of her neck. It was terrifying, yet strangely exciting. Could this be how it happened to April? Raven struggled to break his hold, but it was useless. She was losing her breath now. She tried to calm herself. Maybe he's just playing? went through her mind. She gasped for air. "Vaughn?"

"Uh-huh," Vaughn mimicked her pant.

"You were joking, right?" She could feel herself passing out. There, I said it, she thought. I just accused the boy I love of being a killer.

Vaughn threw Raven down in front of the fire and jumped to his feet. The reflected flame of the fire flickered in Vaughn's eyes. He clenched his fists and spun around, as if he were looking for something to break. Then he stormed off into the pitch-black cabin.

Is this the real Vaughn? Raven wondered. She gulped in huge mouthfuls of air. She heard a crash, and then another, and then silence. She was catching her breath, and her senses were coming back. Suddenly, an anguished shout followed by a tremendous shattering of glass exploded from the other end of the cabin.

11

Raven bolted upright. "Vaughn?" she called into the darkness. "Vaughn! Is that you? Vaughn, where are you?"

"Vaaauuughn!" Raven cried. No one answered.

CHAPTER 2

Hope took another sip of coffee—her third cup of the morning. She'd been up since five, sitting motionless in front of her computer. ARREST RECORDS she typed, watching the words appear on her computer screen. The machine whirred and gave off a sharp beep. ERROR: UNACCEPTABLE CODE flashed at the bottom of the screen.

"Darn!" Hope said out loud. This was all too familiar.

CRIMINALS, she tried. Beep. That wasn't the right code word either. COURT RECORDS. Nope.

She pushed her chair back from her desk and stared at the gray screen. She'd been guessing at words all morning, and she hadn't come up with a thing. Mr. Woolery's police record had to be in there somewhere. Hiding someplace in the information matrix between the computer chips and the modem hookups and the electronic files of the officials of Paradiso, there had to be something about why Mr. Woolery had been arrested and convicted of a crime—a fact Hope had discovered when she successfully tapped into the school records. Now she needed to crack another code. Maybe it would provide a clue to why April had been killed. Hope was desperate to find her cousin's murderer.

But she couldn't even get into the police files, let alone find Mr. Woolery's name in them. It was trial and error. And error. And error.

To make matters much worse, every time Hope typed in a new word, a jolt of panic shot up her neck. The other day as Hope worked at a terminal in the school computer room, she'd gotten a warning message instead of the information she was looking for. STOP SNOOPING, it had said. OR YOU'RE NEXT.

Then, just a night ago, Hope had been chased through the woods by a mysterious, shadowy figure. Her entire body weakened at the memory. She touched her finger to the deep scratch on her skin, where a rock thrown by her stalker had grazed her cheek. If Jess hadn't come to her rescue, she *would* have been next.

A picture forced its way into Hope's mind, a picture that she kept seeing over and over again since the murder. April's arm, lifeless, blue, dangled out of Hope's locker. Hope bit back a cry. For those first few

14

days afterward, she had barely been able to believe her cousin was dead. April, her best friend. April, the most talented artist in Paradiso. April, the Queen of the Peach Blossom Festival. Now the shock was beginning to wear off, and Hope was starting to grasp the truth, deep down in her gut—she'd never see April again. The shock was being replaced by an ache, an emptiness, a longing to at least have been able to say good-bye, to tell April how much she loved her. And occupying the space within her right next to that ache was a driving need to find whoever had done this horrible thing—and put the killer behind bars. Forever.

Every place Hope went in Paradiso reminded her of her cousin—the spot on the school lawn where they used to eat lunch, the white-steepled Church of Christ, where April's father preached, the bench on the town green where they'd hung out in the evenings. Hope and April had joked that the bench was their home in exile. Their families had been feuding since both girls were babies, so neither Hope's house nor April's was a place where they could be together.

Hope's throat tightened in a sob. Maybe it would be easier to be somewhere else altogether—away from Paradiso, away from everything that stirred Hope's memories. She couldn't really blame Spike Navarrone, April's boyfriend, for leaving.

Spike hadn't even been able to wait for the books

15

and other things he'd asked Hope to get for him from his school locker.

Had Spike bolted because the word had gotten out that April was pregnant when she was killed? Was he holding Hope responsible for letting that secret out? That information made Spike a prime suspect.

Hope sighed as she stared at the error message on her computer. GUILTY, she typed in. Even before the machine beeped at her, she knew that word was not going to open any secret files. She prayed that whoever had left the warning message on the school computer didn't have any way of knowing what she was doing at home. It was all such a mess.

She wished Jess were here right now, to hold her and make the bad feelings recede, at least for a while. It had been so wonderful to be with him last night. So tender and warm and exciting. Hope smiled for the first time that morning. He liked her! The hunkiest, nicest guy in school, the star of the Paradiso High swim team liked her! Her, Hope Hubbard! Hope Hubbard and Jess Gardner. She could hardly believe it. Amidst all the horror and sorrow, one good thing had happened.

Only yesterday, a shiver of doubt had remained with Hope about whether Jess could be the killer. But now that he'd held her in his arms as her assailant fled back into the woods, her fears had been put to rest. Now she was free to let her true feelings grow. Now if she shivered, it was from pleasure, as she thought about Jess's embrace. In her mind, she began replaying the kisses they'd shared in the peach orchard last night—the sweet smell of blossoms in the air, her head spinning dizzily, wonderfully . . .

Then she stopped. *Quit daydreaming, Hubbard. You may be in love, but April's killer is still out there. Just waiting to strike again.* Hope thought about being chased through the woods.

She went back to work with a vengeance, punching words into her computer. TOP SECRET. Beep. ERROR: UNACCEPTABLE CODE. CLASSIFIED. Beep. ERROR.

"Hope, sweetie!" Leanne Hubbard's voice was a welcome change of tune from the beeping of Hope's computer. "Come have breakfast! You're going to be late for school." The smell of bacon wafted in from the kitchen.

Her mother was standing over the stove in her nurse's uniform, flipping pancakes and turning the bacon. This was a switch. Normally Hope made her own breakfast, popping a slice of toast in for her mother. Leanne said breakfast was too early to be packing it in like a truck driver, the way Hope did. But since April's murder, Hope's appetite had shrunken away. Her mother had been cooking up Hope's favorite meals to get her to eat again.

Hope came over and peered into the frying pans. Almost against her will, her mouth began to water. It

17

seemed somehow disloyal to April to be getting her appetite back, but that bacon did smell delicious. And the pancakes looked good, too. Hope took a plastic honey bear out of the cupboard to drizzle her favorite topping on her pancakes. It always used to make April mad, the way Hope could eat and eat and never put an extra pound on her rail-thin body.

Leanne flipped the pancakes onto a plate. "What is it you're so busy working on in your room, sweetheart?"

Hope tried to come up with a quick answer. "Oh, just some new stuff on my computer." She couldn't tell her mother that she was trying to come up with clues to April's murder. And she certainly couldn't tell her that she was trying to break into police files. After seeing the cut on Hope's cheek, and hearing about her narrow escape, Leanne had forbidden Hope to do any more investigating. She said it was too dangerous. Besides, any mention of April was certain to make Leanne Hubbard think of Hope's Uncle Ward, or Saint Ward, as April used to call her dad behind his back. Leanne didn't like being reminded of her brother. Especially since he'd been flinging wild accusations about the murder at everybody, including Hope.

Hope was pouring herself a tall glass of orange juice when she heard someone knock at the door. "I'll get it," Leanne said. "You better start breakfast if you want to get to school on time." She ran a hand over her brown hair as she went to the door. "I wonder who that is, so early?" Hope heard her musing as she left the kitchen.

Hope heard her opening the front door. "Well, Jesús—or should I say sheriff?" her mother said.

Hope stopped chewing and dropped her fork. The sheriff was at their door, and in the next room her computer was on, listing all her attempts to break into his confidential files.

"Morning, Leanne," Sheriff Rodriguez said. They had grown up together in Paradiso and were old friends. But this morning, the sheriff was all business. "Is your daughter around? I'd like to talk to her for a moment."

Could Hope sneak into her bedroom and turn off the computer without the sheriff seeing her? Too late. She could hear Leanne showing him into the house and toward the kitchen.

"She's not in some sort of trouble, is she?" Leanne sounded worried.

"Oh, no," the sheriff said. "I just had a couple of questions I wanted to ask her."

Hope felt herself relax a little as the sheriff and her mother came into the kitchen. "Can I make you a cup of coffee?" Leanne offered.

"Thanks, but I've got a lot to do." He turned to Hope. "Good morning, Hope. Nasty cut on your cheek."

Hope touched it. "Sheriff, someone chased me yesterday and threw rocks at me. I think it was April's killer."

Sheriff Rodriguez frowned and took out his little notepad. "Why didn't you report this to me immediately?"

Hope could feel herself blushing. She couldn't very well tell the sheriff that she'd gotten too lost in Jess Gardner's kisses. She shrugged. "I guess I should have." She filled him in on as much as she could. "All I saw was someone in a hooded blue jacket or sweatshirt. The person was too far away to tell anything else."

"And where did this happen?" The sheriff was scribbling down all the information.

"In the woods out by Orchard Road," Hope said.

"Orchard Road? Hmmm. That's near the Navarrones' trailer." The sheriff's expression went from concern to suspicion. "Funny, I'm looking for Carlos. That's what brought me here."

Hope gulped. "Spike? Um, Sheriff, I don't think he's in Paradiso anymore."

"Yes, as soon as he was in the hot seat he left. I was just out there at the trailer. I thought you might know where he went."

Hope turned her palms upward. "I don't know," she said.

The sheriff fixed her with a searching look. "Are you sure?"

Hope nodded. "I'm not all that close to Spike. I mean, we were sort of friends, but through April, you know?"

"Uh-huh." The sheriff nodded. He cast his glance around the kitchen, and Hope saw it settle. She followed it, and her heart jumped into her throat. Her schoolbooks were piled on the end of the kitchen counter—and stacked next to them were Spike's books, the ones Hope hadn't delivered to him the previous night. After her attack, Hope had gone with Jess to Spike's trailer. When his brothers had told her and Jess that Spike was gone, Hope hadn't bothered to go over to the door and leave Spike's things. He wouldn't be coming for them anyway. On the top of the pile was a copy of *Motorcycle World* magazine.

The sheriff went over and picked it up. "Not very friendly with him, huh?" He opened Spike's math book. *Carlos Navarrone*, it said inside the front cover, in letters big enough for Hope to see from across the kitchen. No one called Spike by his real name, but he'd written it the official way inside all his books.

"I—I was bringing those to him," Hope hastened to explain. "That's what I was doing when I got chased. But Spike was already gone."

"I see," the sheriff said. She didn't like the way the sheriff was looking at her, as if she were guilty of

21

something. He poked through the rest of the pile. Then he riffled through Hope's books. As he picked up a worn paperback copy of *Hamlet,* a piece of paper fluttered to the ground.

The note from April! Hope had found it in Spike's locker. She dove for it, but the sheriff grabbed it first.

" 'Meet me at the usual place after dinner tonight,' " he read out loud. "Isn't this April Lovewell's handwriting?"

Hope nodded miserably. She remembered her momentary stab of suspicion when she'd found the note. If Spike and April had met after dinner, she had reasoned, maybe he *was* the killer. Still, deep inside, she didn't believe it. Hope had seen Spike and April together, and she'd known he truly cared for her. She'd also seen the loving, concerned way Spike took care of his two little brothers. But Hope knew the note looked bad.

"Hope Hubbard, did you meet your cousin April on the night of her murder?" Sheriff Rodriguez asked, his voice tight.

Hope was flustered. "You think that note was to *me*?" She shook her head. Then she felt a flicker of guilt. If the note wasn't to her, the sheriff was going to realize it was to Spike. She had just implicated him. Again. First, the sheriff had cornered her into revealing who April's boyfriend was. Now she'd given him what looked like another incriminating piece of evidence.

"Sheriff, I really think Spike is innocent."

The sheriff looked dubious as he fingered the note. "Then why did he leave town? Don't forget there were no signs that April struggled. She must have known her killer pretty well."

Hope let out a long breath. "It was too hard for Spike to be here after April died."

The sheriff arched an eyebrow. "You seem to know a lot about him. For someone who wasn't very close to him," he added. Hope could almost see the word "accomplice" forming in the sheriff's mind. "You wouldn't happen to know where this usual place was where he and your cousin met, would you?"

Hope shook her head. Leanne Hubbard was looking at her with deep lines of concern on her face. "Honey, don't hold anything back. You can tell the sheriff."

Hope tensed with frustration. "But I don't know anything!" If only Spike would come back and answer the sheriff's questions himself. Suddenly, Hope was angry at Spike. It wasn't her fault that the sheriff suspected him. It was Spike's own fault for not facing the questions and clearing his name.

Hope's father had run away long, long ago, when Hope was a baby. To her, running away meant leaving behind people who had to take on all the problems you'd created. That's what Spike had done too. And

23

the worst part is that if the sheriff's busy searching for Spike, he won't be searching as hard for the real killer, Hope thought.

Another knock sounded at the front door. This time, Hope jumped to get it—anything to get away from the sheriff's persistent questions. "Jess!" His blond hair was wet from his morning shower, and his blue polo shirt made his eyes even bluer. The morning began to look brighter.

"What's the sheriff's car doing here?" he asked.

Hope filled him in. "And I'll bet it's going to look even worse when he sees you coming around to visit," she said, lowering her voice to a whisper. Jess had been the target of a tornado of rumors over the past few days, with Penny Bolton, the biggest mouth at Paradiso High, fueling the storm. Hope now knew that all the talk was just hot air. But the sheriff was going to need to be convinced.

"Maybe I should leave before he sees me," Jess whispered back.

Hope shook her head. "Maybe you should face him and get it over with. Jess, you're innocent. You've got to make sure the sheriff knows that." She wished she could tell Spike the same thing.

"Yeah. You're right." Jess leaned close to Hope. "But first, I forgot to say a proper good morning." He bent even closer and drew her into a kiss.

"Good morning to you, too," Hope whispered.

Jess kissed her once more. "Okay. Now I'm ready to face him."

Leanne and the sheriff were standing around uncomfortably in the kitchen. They didn't look like old friends anymore. The sheriff looked at Jess, and Hope could see Jess tense up.

But the sheriff extended his hand cordially. "Son, perhaps I was guilty of listening to rumors. Maybe you're not our man after all. It seems our man has skipped town."

Hope wanted to come to Spike's defense, but she didn't. She bit her lip and kept quiet. At least Jess appeared to be off the hook.

"I don't know about that, but I do know I'm not your man," Jess said. "That rope and wrench everybody was talking about are from my dad's shop."

"I'm glad to know that, son," Sheriff Rodriguez said. "You wouldn't mind if I took them in to have some tests done?"

"No, sir. Not at all, sir," Jess said formally. "They're in the trunk of my car. It's open."

"And just for the record," the sheriff said, "do you by any chance wear a $10\frac{1}{2}$ C sneaker?"

Everyone in the kitchen looked at Jess's feet. Hope and Jess started laughing. "They say I win swim meets because I have built-in flippers," Jess kidded. The sheriff and Hope's mom laughed too.

But Hope stopped laughing as she realized what the

sheriff was referring to: the half footprint in the mud outside the back door to the school, where the killer had gotten in. "They got the analysis back on the plaster cast?" she asked the sheriff.

He nodded. "The print was too washed out to get a make on it, but it looks to be a size 10 1/2 men's sneaker. Well. I'll let you folks finish your breakfast. Sorry to disturb you." He sounded more like the easygoing, friendly sheriff of little Paradiso again.

But as he turned to go, Sheriff Rodriguez pocketed April's note to Spike.

Exhibit *A*, Hope thought. With me as a possible accomplice. And the real murderer still after me.

CHAPTER 3

"You look very pretty today, Señorita Pinkerton. Yes, very beautiful." Manuel, the chauffeur and handyman, greeted Lacey in front of the family mansion with a warm smile. He had her red Ferrari waiting for her. As he opened the door on the driver's side, he tipped his cap and smiled, ever so humbly.

Lacey returned the smile. "Thank you, Manuel. It's a nice day, isn't it?" she replied.

Manuel was startled. "Excuse me, señorita?"

This was not the Lacey he was used to. Normally she hopped in her car and took off without even saying good morning. On most mornings, Lacey enjoyed another episode of princess versus humble servant. She would get a laugh out of racing the car down the driveway and blowing exhaust in Manuel's face as he bowed graciously before her.

But today, Manuel's friendly tone had struck a

chord in Lacey. Since breaking up with Vaughn and then losing the Peach Blossom contest—at least the first time around—she had been feeling extremely low. She hadn't heard nearly enough compliments recently. Oh, maybe from the scores of geeks and nerds that were always drooling over her in school. But that was different. Somehow, hearing it from Manuel, impeccably dressed in his black uniform, a white carnation in his lapel, it seemed genuine and respectful.

"I said, it's a beautiful day, Manuel. Beau-ti-ful. Well, isn't it?" she repeated, only this time with a touch of sarcasm. "Manuel, you've got to practice your English!"

Now that was the Lacey he was more accustomed to.

"Yes, ma'am. *Sí, sí.* I practice my English. Yes, of course. I'm sorry," he apologized.

"Anyway, thank you for your compliment. You like my new dress? Daddy brought it from Paris. It's the latest." She proudly showed off the new outfit, an alarmingly short cotton minidress. The fabric was a collaged print of maps of the world in an array of soft, pale colors.

Lacey pretended she was parading down the runway, hundreds of eyes gazing at her, flashbulbs popping, as she modeled the dress for Manuel right there in her driveway. She heard him applauding as she twirled about, letting the dress catch in the breeze and hover like a parachute. Just like the videos of Parisian fashion shows she'd seen in the Sacramento boutiques.

"So nice to see you happy, señorita." Manuel motioned to the opened car door. "But don't be late for school, Señorita Lacey."

Damn. Lacey's smile became a frown as she plummeted back down to earth. At the mere mention of Paradiso High, all the people and problems that went along with it came into sharp focus. "Thanks a lot, Manuel," she said, disenchanted.

Lacey got into the car, slammed the door, turned on the engine, revved up, and took off, attacking the narrow curves of Winding Hill Road at top speed.

As she whizzed past the De Santis house, Lacey grimaced. Yesterday Kiki had been her best friend, today they were enemies. And all because of the Peach Blossom contest.

The nerve of Kiki to think she could win Pretty Peggy Sue over me, Lacey thought. She barely wanted to be in the contest anyway. Why didn't she just quit like she promised?

Lacey had been confident when she'd planted the idea in Kiki's head—okay, pressured her—to withdraw from the contest. And it had almost worked. But almost didn't count. Now, with April dead and Lacey's friendship with Kiki on the rocks, Lacey wondered if there was any hope that the Peach Blossom contest could ever be any fun. What had happened to that picture-perfect story where the town of Paradiso cheered mightily for Lacey as she paraded down Old Town Road, Peach Blossom Queen and soon-to-be movie star?

Why did it have to happen this way? she asked herself. This contest was supposed to be the highlight of my senior year. Instead it's ruined my life. I miss Kiki. She was my best friend in the world. Hanging out with Kiki at her pool helped me forget all my problems with Mother and Daddy. Ever since the contest and April's murder everything with her has been so messed up. I wish we could be friends again. Lacey even found herself considering picking Kiki up so that they could go to Rosa's Café for a morning iced tea, the way they used to.

But she drove right by the house. Kiki can come to me and make up, she thought. Besides, she figured that Kiki had already gotten a ride from Vaughn, who had been driving her to Rosa's ever since he started dating Raven.

Vaughn, Kiki, and Raven. Lacey's ex-boyfriend, ex-best friend, and worst nightmare. Lacey got furious just thinking about the three of them hanging out together. The Vaughn and Raven thing was bad enough. Lacey knew that Vaughn was happy to be with Raven anywhere. Whether it was at her parents' café during the breakfast shift, at a SCAM meeting, discussing political tactics, or in the lunchroom over a meat loaf w/mashed potatoes, it didn't matter.

The town had recently lost April Lovewell, but Lacey had lost a lot more than that. Her boyfriend, her best friend, and the Peach Blossom contest.

Well, at least I still have a second chance at the contest, she thought. Don't give up on me, Hollywood.

But the emptiness in her stomach told her that her friendship with Kiki just might be as important. And it wouldn't be so bad to have a boyfriend, either. Who ever heard of the hottest girl in the school—a senior, no less—being single in the spring?

Lacey screeched to a halt at the intersection of Winding Hill and Old Town roads, making a point to stop completely at the blinking red light, just in case Sheriff Rodriguez was waiting there, eager as usual to hand her another summons. Lacey was convinced that the town traffic department would be broke if it weren't for her.

Not today, Rodriguez. No way. Lacey scowled.

As she turned onto Old Town Road, she noticed that Kiki was standing at the bus stop, waiting. She was alone.

Lacey was sure Kiki was looking at her through those sunglasses. Kiki had a book open and was pretending to read, but Lacey knew she was actually

31

watching the Ferrari. Lacey waved from across the street, and Kiki suddenly turned away.

Fine, Lacey thought. If she's gonna ignore me, I'll blow right by her. Ticket or not.

As Lacey whipped past the bus stop, she was extra careful not to turn her head even the slightest bit toward Kiki. But a little farther down the road Lacey screeched to a stop. Kiki's gonna make up with me if it kills her, Lacey decided.

Lacey backed up the Ferrari and came to a halt in front of Kiki. She watched Kiki take a giant step backward.

"Since when does a girl from the Hill take the bus to school? I thought we were above that. Come on, Kiki, I'll drive you." Lacey waited.

No response. She watched Kiki stubbornly ignore her, flipping a page in the book. Kiki was developing a serious attitude problem.

"How about an iced tea at Rosa's? You owe me for last time." No response. "Come on, I'm dying for one. How 'bout it, Kiki? Keeks? Come on, babe. Hop in. Look, I'll tell you what. I'll even let you drive. . . ." Lacey was sure that would work.

Still nothing. Not even the slightest sign that she had been listening. Kiki kept her head buried in her book, refusing to even acknowledge Lacey's existence. *Cold.*

Lacey shut off the engine. She got out of the car

32

and walked up close to Kiki, who had backed into a corner of the bus shelter. An occasional hum of a passing car and two birds chirping in the eucalyptus tree that helped shade the bus stop were the only sounds around them.

"Hey, Kiki," Lacey tried again, "remember me? Lacey. Remember your best friend and fellow Pink? It's me, Lacey!" she shouted.

Finally Kiki turned around and faced Lacey. She pushed the sunglasses up on top of her head and gave Lacey a long, hard stare.

"If looks could kill . . ." Lacey was starting to regret having made the effort. Especially since Kiki should have come begging to *her.*

"You know, Lacey," Kiki said sharply, "just yesterday, I was gonna back out of the contest. Not because I couldn't handle it, but for you. Because I know how important it is to you. Because you are my best friend . . . *were* my best friend!"

Lacey felt a stab of hurt.

Kiki continued. "But after what your mother did to me last night, I've changed my mind. I'm more determined than ever to win. Just so you won't."

Darla! Really, it would be better for everyone—especially Lacey—if they just stopped letting Darla leave the house. But Lacey had no idea what her mother had done this time. "My mother? Kiki . . . I don't know what . . ."

33

"Don't play innocent with me, Lacey Pinkerton! You're forgetting how well I know you and your family. All the dirty tricks you have up your sleeves," Kiki snapped. "If you think you and your mom are gonna get away with it, you're wrong. I'm not gonna let you intimidate me anymore. Just stay away from me!"

Lacey was shocked. Kiki never acted this way, especially toward her. She was usually so careful not to bad-mouth other people. What had happened to sweet, friendly Kiki De Santis? What could have sent her off the deep end like this? Lacey couldn't imagine.

"I really wish I knew what you were talking about. My mother? What did she do?" Lacey asked. "Seriously, Kiki, what's going on?"

But Kiki continued her attack. "Give it up, Lacey. You know exactly what she did. And I know you put her up to it. You'd do anything to win Peggy Sue."

What *had* her mother done? "If you're going to go around making accusations about my family, you'd better at least tell me what they are." Lacey took a step closer to Kiki, forcing her against the wall of the bus shelter.

Kiki took a deep breath. "Or else what, Lacey? Are you threatening me too? Isn't having your mother do it enough? Why don't you just go away? I'm sick of your constant bullying. You and your whole family are all the same. Well, I'm not gonna stand for it anymore. Just keep away from me, Lacey!" She pushed

Lacey away from her and moved out from the corner of the bus shelter.

Lacey felt herself stumble. "Don't you ever touch me!" She unfurled all her fury at Kiki, reaching out and pushing her back.

Kiki threw her book on the ground, almost hitting Lacey's leg. Lacey grabbed Kiki's sunglasses from the top of her head and flung them out onto the street. Kiki retaliated by pushing Lacey again, hard against the bus stop bench, making her fall to the ground.

There was a long, cold silence. Lacey's heart was pounding and her head was spinning. She struggled to her feet. She looked Kiki dead in the eye. "Say whatever you want about me, De Santis. But leave my family alone. If I ever hear you talking about my parents—"

"You don't scare me, Lacey." Kiki glared back. "I don't know why you even bothered to stop here. I'll bet you just wanted to make my day start off miserably. Well, it worked."

Lacey felt her anger spiraling. "You know, Kiki, I came here to patch things up. I was even ready to forgive you for staying in the contest when you promised me you'd drop out. I thought our friendship was a little more important to you. But I guess not. Just forget it, Kiki. You're not worth it."

Kiki's eyes welled up. Lacey could see she was fighting, unsuccessfully, to hold back tears. "I don't believe you, Lacey. Not for a second. You're up to something. As usual. I'm not falling for your sweetness act ever again. It makes me sick."

"You're crazy." Lacey had had enough for one morning. She had never gotten this much abuse from anybody. Except Daddy. But outside of the house, Lacey had never been treated like this.

Lacey turned away from Kiki, trying to ignore the sound of her crying. She brushed off some of the dirt that had gotten on her new dress. She got back in her car and started the engine. In the rearview mirror, she noticed Winston Purdy riding up on his bike.

"Looks like the bus isn't coming," she called to Kiki. "Might as well hop on the nerd's handlebars. That's about your speed."

Winston rode by on his rickety bike and waved to them, but they were too caught up in their fight to wave back. Lacey shot Kiki a final glare. She drove off without another look, leaving Kiki alone in tears. Good.

But Kiki's talk about Darla had left Lacey in a panic. What had her mother done? What could she possibly want with Kiki?

Then it hit her. The Peach Blossom contest. What else could it be? Darla had worn the crown herself, about a million years ago, and she had made it more than obvious that she would be furious if Lacey lost. "You *will* win, won't you?" she'd said coldly. Lacey remembered her words exactly. Winning was even more important to Darla than to Lacey. Was her mother trying to increase Lacey's odds by terrifying Kiki into quitting? Lacey knew it was something Darla was quite capable of. How far would she go? . . . How far had she gone already?

April Lovewell had been the first person to get in the way of Lacey's winning. April was dead.

CHAPTER 4

"Good morning, boys and girls," Principal Appleby said into the microphone onstage. His gangly legs stuck out of the bottom of his trousers, and he blinked myopically behind his horn-rimmed glasses.

"Good morning, Mr. Appleby," Kiki said automatically, the voices around her echoing the greeting in unison.

"Boys and girls . . ." he began, fidgeting with a piece of paper in one hand and running the other through the few strands of hair that covered his pink scalp.

"Boys and girls? Poisoned squirrels?" someone yelled from the audience. Everyone cracked up. Onstage, Mr. Appleby gave a nervous chuckle.

"Ahem, all right, then. Poisoned squirrels . . ." No wonder everyone called him Dwight the Dweeb.

Kiki groaned and leaned over to Bobby Deeter. "Isn't he ever going to learn to get to the point?"

"Who'd we make fun of if he did?" Bobby whispered back.

"Guys and gals, I've called this special assembly to announce the rescheduling of the Paradiso Peach Blossom Festival and Ball," Mr. Appleby said.

Applause broke out from various parts of the auditorium. It was loudest from the section where Lacey was holding court. Kiki could see her surrounded by her two faithful sidekicks, Renée Henderson and Penny Bolton, and a number of guys who would clearly die for a chance to take Lacey to the Festival Ball. Kiki shot Lacey her dirtiest look.

"I, ah, I'm happy the festival is back on, too," Mr. Appleby said. The end of his sentence was swallowed in the earsplitting squeal of the loudspeaker system. Kiki covered her ears. Mr. Appleby tapped the microphone several times. "Ah, where was I? Ah, yes. We're all happy about the festival. But I don't think we can go ahead without a mention of our dear friend and classmate, April Lovewell."

The auditorium grew silent. The shuffling and coughing and restlessness was snuffed out by the shadow of murder.

"I know how much April's death has affected us all," Mr. Appleby said, "and I'm sure none of us will forget that she was supposed to be presiding over the Peach Blossom Ball as our Queen."

Kiki sneaked another look at Lacey. She saw Lacey grimace. Lacey certainly wasn't going to forget that she'd lost to April. And neither would her mother. Darla Pinkerton had come by while Kiki was in the pool yesterday.

"It might be a smart idea to drop out. If you know what's good for you," Mrs. Pinkerton had threatened. Lacey was just like her. She had to be in on it.

"I want you all to know," Mr. Appleby was saying, "that we're forming an April Lovewell Memorial Foundation, on the suggestion of one of our Peach Blossom Queen hopefuls, Kiki De Santis."

There was a sprinkling of applause. Kiki blushed, pushing aside her thoughts of Lacey and her mother.

Mr. Appleby went on. "I know I speak for all of us in Paradiso when I say we're going to miss April."

All of us except the killer, Kiki thought. She felt a sudden wave of anxiety crash over her. Maybe the killer was right here, in this room. The news was spreading all over school that Hope Hubbard had been chased through the woods by someone yesterday, and she had a nasty scratch on her face to show for it. Was the murderer after victim number two?

"But we've made a decision to celebrate life," Mr. Appleby continued. "April's memory will be with us, and I'm sure she would have joined us in reveling in

40

the joy of spring and the glory of our orchards bearing fruit, and the company of our cherished friends . . ."

A few kids snickered as Mr. Appleby embarrassed himself with the prepared speech he was reading from.

"Lacey for Queen!" shouted a deep voice from the direction of Lacey's entourage. "The Queen is dead! Long live the Queen!"

A mixture of laughter and shocked gasps sounded around the auditorium. Kiki couldn't understand the people who were laughing. It was as if they wanted to cover up the gruesome reality of April's murder. It was too ugly, too scary. Instead, they'd turned it into a sick joke, a topic of hot gossip, a made-for-TV movie.

On stage, Mr. Appleby finished his ode to the Peach Blossom Festival. "And so, boys and—ah, ladies and gentlemen, the Peach Blossom Festival will be held the weekend after this one." Cheers and applause. "The ball will be that Saturday." More applause. "And next week, we will announce the Queen." Whistles, loudest cheers. "I'm sure the three lovely hopefuls need no introduction. But I'm going to introduce them anyway." Mr. Appleby cackled at his own joke. "They are: Lacey Pinkerton!"

Lacey stood up and gave her Hollywood smile—the one where she pulled the corners of her mouth back and showed all those teeth. To the sound of boisterous cheers, she waved her hand over her head as if she'd already been crowned.

"Kiki De Santis!" Mr. Appleby called.

Bobby gave Kiki a little nudge. She stood up and grinned. As she sat back down, Bobby whispered, "You're going to be the most beautiful Queen." He gave her a kiss on the cheek, his brown eyes warm.

Kiki rumpled the top of Bobby's straight, thick dark hair. "Maybe," she said. Bobby was so sweet, and he cared for her so much. She wished she could be as there for him as he was for her. But lately her feelings had begun to change, and she didn't know what to do about it. Bobby would be crushed if she broke up with him. But that's what her heart was telling her to do.

"And the last of our three lovely ladies is Raven Cruz," Mr. Appleby said. Kiki looked around the auditorium for Raven. She didn't stand up.

"Raven?" Mr. Appleby said. "Has anyone seen Raven today?" No one answered. "Well, ah, um, you all probably know her from her work on SCAM."

"Maybe one of the mall people cemented her over!" a big voice boomed out. Kiki knew that voice. Its owner was equally big—and obnoxious. Eddie Hagenspitzel. With murder on everyone's lips, Kiki didn't think Eddie's attempt at humor was very funny.

Mr. Appleby cleared his throat. "It's going to be a tough decision. I'd like to see all three of these young

42

ladies win. Yes, I would be honored to have each one of them reigning over our parade with grace and charm and—"

Fortunately, Mr. Appleby's speech was interrupted by Ms. Nyhart, his secretary. She walked to the middle of the stage and handed him a note, which he unfolded and read. A look of worry appeared on his face. "Ah, if anyone does see Raven Cruz, she is to call home immediately." His voice dropped. "Hmm. So she's not at home, either." Mr. Appleby's musings were broadcast across the auditorium.

A hum spread through the auditorium as rumors ignited. Raven wasn't in school. Neither was Vaughn, who hadn't come by to give Kiki a lift to school that morning.

A chill shook Kiki's whole body. Raven and Vaughn were missing. And there was a murderer loose.

CHAPTER 5

The Blue Hawaii. The name conjured up images of endless surf, white sand, and palm trees. Unless you were from Paradiso. Then it meant darkness and dinginess, the smell of sour beer, a place you only went if you were looking for trouble.

"Maybe we should just wait until we can talk to Mrs. Navarrone at home," Hope said to Jess as they drove toward the bar. "Anyway, are we going to have time? Lunchtime's half over."

"Hope, from what I've heard, Spike's mom pretty much lives at the Blue Hawaii. If we want to find Spike, we'd better not wait. We'll get back to school on time."

"Yeah. Okay," Hope said. It had been all over school after the assembly that Sheriff Rodriguez had put out a statewide all-points bulletin on Spike. Any officer who saw him was to pick him up and bring him in for questioning. If Spike hadn't done anything wrong before, he was doing it now, by fleeing from the law.

"We've gotta get Spike back here to clear everything up," Hope said. Unless he can't clear things up, she thought. She remembered what she'd discovered that morning. She almost didn't want to tell Jess, for fear of hearing herself say it out loud. It made Spike seem so guilty. "Jess?"

"Uh-huh?" Jess turned onto Old Town Road and picked up speed.

"You know how I went to turn off my computer after the sheriff left?" Hope asked. Jess nodded. "Well, before I did, I pulled up the questionnaires for my computer dating service."

"You did? Why?"

"Well, remember the part where you had to put down hat size, shoe size, favorite flower, and all that other stuff, in case your date wanted to buy you a present?"

"Sure do," Jess said. "Boy, was Lacey mad that I filled out one of those forms." Lacey and Jess had dated before she'd gone out with Vaughn.

"Lacey probably wanted to kill Denise Guthrie, huh?"

"You remember that I got matched up with Denise?" Jess shook his head and laughed.

"Well, I kind of wished you'd get matched up with

me," Hope said. She could feel her cheeks growing warm.

"Should have. I mean, not that I took Denise out anyway. Lacey would have made my life miserable. But what about those questionnaires?" Jess asked.

"Well . . . I pulled up Spike's." Hope hesitated for a moment. "And—Jess, he wears a size ten-and-a-half shoe."

The car was filled with tense silence. Then Jess said uneasily, "Well, I'm sure lots of guys do."

Hope nodded. "Yeah, twenty-three of the people who filled out questionnaires. Bubba Dole was one of them."

"Psycho's a better bet for the murderer than Spike," Jess said.

"I know," Hope agreed. "Still . . ."

"Well, we just have to find him," Jess said. "Whether he's guilty or not." His voice sounded funny and tight, as if he didn't want to believe the worst about Spike either.

Neither Hope nor Jess said anything for a few minutes. Hope looked out the window. It was a beautiful day. Another beautiful day. It had been like this practically every day since April's murder. Hope wished it would rain. Maybe it would wash away the evil that seemed to infest every fragrant, blossoming tree.

Jess turned right onto Maplewood Drive. The steeple of Uncle Ward's church split the sky. As they got closer, Hope saw that her uncle was out front, pruning some bushes. She ducked beneath the dashboard as they drove by. With a father like Saint Ward, no wonder April had to meet Spike in a secret place. As she crouched in the seat of Jess's car, Hope found herself wondering where that place had been.

"Hey, I thought you wanted to end the fight between your mom and the Lovewells," Jess said, giving Hope's long brown hair a little tug.

"I do," said Hope. "Are we past him yet?"

"Coast's clear. But I don't see how the way to make peace is to hide every time you see the guy, Hope."

Hope poked her head up cautiously. She felt a little dumb. "I know. But he hates me so much—it's just easiest to avoid him."

"You wanna know what I think?" Jess said. "You and your mom ought to march right in there in the middle of one of the reverend's sermons on peace and brotherhood. Maybe he'd put two and two together and get the message."

Hope sighed. "I wish. But I don't think he's going to be feeling too brotherly until they find April's killer. And maybe not after that, either." She turned around in her seat. Uncle Ward was a tiny dark figure against the lush green lawn of the church. "I wonder what size shoe *he* wears," Hope said.

Jess rounded another corner and the church disappeared from view, except for the spire, poking up behind the houses they drove past. "You mean maybe he found out April was pregnant . . ." Jess said.

Hope let out a long sigh. "I don't know what I mean anymore," she said. "I'm so tired."

Jess reached out with one hand and kneaded the tight muscles around Hope's left shoulder. A tingle went through her at his touch. She still couldn't quite believe that she was with Jess Gardner. She closed her eyes and concentrated on his caresses.

But the tension in her shoulders came rushing back as the car bumped over the train tracks, and a few moments later, Jess turned onto Route 4 and pulled up to the Blue Hawaii.

The paint was peeling off the low, dilapidated building, and a sharp, stale odor surrounded it like a moat. One of the windows had been broken and was now boarded up with a graffiti-covered plank of rotten plywood. A faded sign over the door announced the name of the bar, with a picture of a wave swelling over the letters. The wave, probably once turquoise, had faded to a sick green-yellow. It looked like the kind of place where a murderer would hang out.

Hope got out of the car and wrinkled her nose. Jess came around and slipped his hand into hers. It made walking through the door of the awful place a little easier.

Hope blinked several times to adjust her eyes to the dimness. It wasn't hard to find Mrs. Navarrone. There were four people in the bar. Two men at a rickety, sticky-looking table. The bartender, a short man with a shaved head and his arms covered with tattoos. And Spike's mom, skinny, unkempt, her dark hair a mess, half slumped over a can of beer at the end of the bar. A cigarette burned in one hand.

"Mrs. Navarrone?" Jess said. He and Hope approached her. She looked at them blankly. "I'm Jess Gardner. A friend of Spike's. I was out at the trailer once. This is Hope Hubbard."

Hope had known Mrs. Navarrone since she was little, but Spike's mom gave no sign of recognition. She stared at them and took a swig of beer. "Yeah?"

"We—we're looking for Spike," Hope ventured.

"Gone." Mrs. Navarrone banged down her beer can as if to emphasize the finality of it.

"We know," Jess said. "But we thought you might know where."

"I don't know, and I don't care," Mrs. Navarrone said. "I told the sheriff just this morning." Hope and Jess exchanged glances. "But if any of you find him," Mrs. Navarrone went on, her words slurred, "you tell him to kiss off. Tell him his mama said to kiss off. Leaving me all alone to do ever'thing by myself."

Hope tried not to breathe too hard. The air was so foul in the Blue Hawaii. Simultaneous waves of disgust and pity for Mrs. Navarrone washed over her. "So you don't have any idea where he went?"

Mrs. Navarrone waved her hand. The cigarette ash fell to the floor. "Probably halfway to Tijuana by now. That's where they all go when they're running from the law."

Hope felt her breath catch. Even Spike's own mother thought he was hiding from the police. She saw Jess's mouth turn down too. Was Spike really guilty?

"I wonder if there is anyone he was especially close to," Jess said. "A relative or something?"

"Yeah. His dad. Behind bars. But I doubt he's gonna visit him in the slammer. At least not on his own. No. He'll wait till they send him there. He'll have plenty of time then to hang out with his old man." Spike's mother let out a drunken laugh. There wasn't a drop of amusement in it.

"Well, um, thank you for your help, Mrs. Navarrone." Another brittle laugh crackled mirthlessly in the stale air.

Hope and Jess turned to leave. Mrs. Navarrone ordered herself another beer.

CHAPTER 6

Who killed Peggy Sue? Why April? Where are Raven and Vaughn? Who's next? What's for lunch?

If you were lying on the grass out on the back lawn of Paradiso High listening to all the chatter, you would get a million and one answers to each question —except the one about the lunch menu. Everyone knew Thursday meant franks 'n' beans w/ fruit cup. Lacey and her entourage usually brought their lunch from home on Thursdays.

Lacey was basking in the midday sun, hanging out with Penny and Renée, the remaining members of the Pinks. She slid the straps of her dress down to avoid tan lines on her shoulders. Always a perfect tan for Lacey. Penny and Renée had both pulled their shirts up as far as they dared to tan their stomachs. Renée's was starting to turn as red as her hair, and a few new freckles showed on her pretty face. In contrast,

Penny's skin was a smooth, even brown and getting darker fast. They were all ignoring the constant whistles and catcalls directed at them. But they kept their ears open to any new gossip that might come their way, especially about the murder.

"Weird," Lacey said. "Just plain weird."

"Sort of like the twilight zone around here, isn't it?" Renée commented. "Anyone want the rest of my cottage cheese and fruit? I'm on a diet."

"Here, I'll trade you for the rest of my lobster salad. I've had it two days in a row." Lacey handed Renée a plastic container filled with large chunks of lobster meat and a thick, creamy dressing.

"Wow, thanks, Lacey," said Renée, attacking the lobster salad with relish.

"It *is* like the twilight zone," Lacey said. "I wonder who's gonna play me in the film version."

"If you win the Peach Blossom contest, you can play yourself!" Penny bit into a giant ham-and-Swiss sandwich.

"I wonder who'd get to play April?" added Renée, wiping a glob of mayo from her cheek.

"Who cares?" Penny said. "Everyone is making such a big deal about April, who was a total nobody two weeks ago. She's more popular dead than alive."

"Look," Lacey said, pointing to the back door, which now had a giant metal chain wrapped around it. "That's where they say the murderer got in.

Creepy. It would take Houdini to get through there now."

"Speaking of famous disappearing acts, where do you think Vaughn and Raven are?" Renée asked. "Think something's up?"

"Yeah. Something's up," Lacey snapped. "Raven stole my boyfriend. That's what's up."

"I think you're lucky, Lacey," Penny remarked. "I wonder about him," she said, raising her eyebrows.

"What's that supposed to mean, Pen?" Lacey asked warily. "You know something that we don't?"

"Well . . ."

"I know that look, Penny. You think that Vaughn's—"

"A maniac killer," Penny said matter-of-factly. "That's right. It's a possibility. And for all we know, he's after Raven right now."

"Come on," Renée said doubtfully. "Vaughn Cutter?"

"Think about it," Penny said sharply. "He's got a seriously bad temper. He's always beating people up when he's ticked off at something. Let's face it. He's scary."

"Mmmm. He's so cute when he gets mad," Lacey said with a guilty grin. "He gets all red in the face. So sexy. I love it."

"Yeah, but he could be dangerous, Lacey," Penny said.

"Dangerously cute and delicious. Just the way I like 'em," Lacey remarked. Like the wild time she had had with Vaughn at his family's lakeside cabin in Hidden Valley. She and Vaughn had a mammoth argument that night. He was so livid that he'd bashed a hole in the cabin wall. But it was the way the night ended that made it so memorable. The make-up scene was more furious than the fight. Lacey could still feel every passionate kiss they had shared in front of the fireplace. She didn't mind being vulnerable to Vaughn's temper if it meant winding up wrapped in a blanket with him in front of a crackling fire.

"I don't know, Lacey," Renée said. "Penny's got a point. I've seen his fists fly. He gets pretty scary. He *is* missing, you know. And so is Raven. And her parents are looking for her. They're obviously worried about something. What if . . ."

"Poor Raven," Penny said, gesturing toward the chained door.

"Just because Raven's not in school today doesn't mean we have to put her in her grave and bury her already," Lacey said. Not that it would be the worst thing in the world. At least I'd have an easier time winning the Peach Blossom contest. And Daddy's mall project would go through without a fight.

"Maybe you're right, Lacey," Renée said. "We can't be so sure. Besides, Vaughn and Raven aren't the only ones missing. I don't see Hope and Jess around anywhere. Where do you think they're off to?"

"Probably celebrating Jess's freedom. They're out in some haystack making out," Lacey said with a note of bitterness.

Renée wrapped her arms around herself and made kissing noises. "Hope and Jess. True love at last," she said

"Shut up, Renée," Lacey warned.

"Oops. Sorry, Lacey. I was only kidding." Renée turned beet red. "I didn't mean it."

"She doesn't deserve Jess. Not for a second. That little snoop." Lacey remembered the horrible sight of the two, smiling at each other like newlyweds, in front of Radio Shack. It was unbearable to see Jess with someone else. Especially Hope. Lacey was sorry she had ever broken up with Jess.

"That's some scratch she's got on her face," she added. "I don't know how Jess can stand to look at her now. Not that she was ever good looking."

"Hope's telling people Jess saved her from the killer," Renée said.

"Well, I wouldn't listen to anything Hope said." Penny seemed annoyed. "For all we know, it was Jess who beaned her with the rock. Maybe she's covering up for him. Besides, she's a jerk. Right, Lacey?"

"You know how I feel about that little . . ."

"Why are you guys so harsh?" Renée asked. "I

don't get it. She's not *that* bad. And I don't know why you're still so hung up on Jess, Lacey. I seem to remember it was *you* who broke up with *him.*"

"So . . ." Lacey said.

"So, you should forget about him. Plenty of other fish in the sea. That's what you always said."

"Yeah, but he's the best swimmer of them all. Believe me." Lacey managed a laugh.

Lacey plucked a handful of wildflowers from the lawn, idly arranging them into a little bouquet. She leaned into them to get their gentle scent . . . and instantly felt a sneeze coming on. She reached for her pink handkerchief in the pocket of her—"Achoooo!"

Before she'd even gotten her hand into the pocket of her shoulder bag, Eddie Hagenspitzel appeared from nowhere. He knelt down in front of Lacey and stuck his arm out in front of her face.

"Here, Lacey. Sorry that I don't have a handkerchief, but feel free to use my sleeve. One hundred percent cotton."

Renée and Penny were in stitches. They clearly thought Eddie was the funniest kid in the school.

"Don't be so dumb, Hagenspitzel," Lacey snapped. "You think I'd wipe *my* nose on *your* sleeve? Gross. Get a life." Eddie got up and left.

"He's a fool," Lacey said nastily to Penny and Renée, but loudly enough for Eddie to overhear.

"Pretty mean, Lacey," Penny remarked.

"Why so hard, Lacey?" Renée asked. "He was only joking around. You know his style."

"Not worth wasting my time on. You know? Besides, he's fat and ugly." Lacey faked a yawn. "And his humor is so juvenile. Let's change the subject. Weren't we talking about all the missing people in Paradiso?"

"I thought you didn't want to talk about Vaughn and Raven or Jess and Hope," Renée said.

"I don't. But what about Spike? Where's he hiding out? Sure would like to know." Lacey wondered what tricks the biker was up to.

"I'll bet he's south of the border. It'll be hard to find him in Mexico," Renée said.

"Hanging out on some sunny beach in Acapulco. Wish I were there with him. Not a bad life for a murderer," Lacey kidded. "I think he's innocent anyway." Lacey studied Penny's and Renée's faces to gauge their reactions. "I know what that means, Penny. So Vaughn's the murderer and Spike's the murderer too?"

"Well, he always scared me. All that revving up his bike and giving creepy looks to everyone," she said. "You don't put out an APB for nothing, you know."

Lacey shook her head. "I thought you read murder mysteries all the time. When are the police ever right?"

"It's true," Renée agreed. "Sheriff Rodriguez can

barely chew gum and write Lacey a speeding ticket at the same time. Still, I wouldn't want to be the one to find Spike hiding in some dark alley. If he killed once, he could do it again."

Lacey objected. "Spike wouldn't kill the woman he loved. Especially when she was carrying his baby. He's too cool to resort to murder. If he didn't want to play daddy for the rest of his life, he'd just split. But murder?"

"Someone had to do it," Renée said.

"You guys think everyone did it." Lacey started counting on her fingers. "Yesterday it was Jess. Today it's either Vaughn or Spike. Or even Raven or Hope. And don't forget Mr. Woolery, Bubba Dole, Willa Flicker, or even the Dweeb. You guys are going overboard. Everyone can't be a psychopath."

"So who did do it, then?" Penny challenged. "Who killed April?"

"I don't know, but I'm sure the real murderer is lurking around, going totally unsuspected, just waiting to strike again," Lacey answered, scaring herself a little at the suggestion. She thought about her confrontation with Kiki earlier, and Kiki's frightening accusations about Darla. At least her mother wasn't on the list of suspects. Not yet.

"Aren't you worried for yourself, Lacey?" Renée asked. "What if the killer is just waiting for the next

Peach Blossom Queen to be announced? I'd be freaked if I were you."

"I guess I am, but I'm better off dead than showing up at the ball without a date." Lacey sighed. "Maybe I could convince him to escort me to the dance before he tightens the noose . . . or after, just so long as I'm not dateless."

"Gross! I think you're taking it too lightly, Lacey." Renée looked at Penny. "I think we should take turns watching out for Lacey until the murderer is found."

Penny waved her hand. "Lacey will be fine. I know it. April Lovewell was a nothing. And now she's less than nothing. Nobody in his right mind would dare try to hurt Lacey."

Lacey gave Penny a squeeze. She was so loyal.

"Yeah, but what if the killer's not in his right mind?" Renée asked.

Penny gave a sharp frown. "Give it a break, Renée."

"Yeah, let's talk about something else," Lacey agreed. "Like where I'm going to get a hot date for the ball. After all, he'll be chaperoning the Queen of Paradiso." Lacey looked around to see if she spotted any potential candidates lying out on the grass. "Absolutely no one."

"How about Winston?" Renée pointed to Winston Purdy III, nerd of nerds, sitting alone on a rock, reading. "I think behind those horn rims he's really cute. And a sweetie pie."

"Sure. He'll be great during milk and cookies time. Then we can take our naps." Lacey couldn't believe the suggestion.

"You never know, Lacey," Renée remarked. "Sometimes the nerds turn out to be the coolest of all. Like a lot of artists and musicians."

"Come on, guys, we're talking Winston Purdy the third!" Lacey gave a second look at Winston. He really was such a geek. She remembered the secret valentine she had gotten from him. Pretty easy to figure out who it was from since it was written on the back of his math homework. Advanced calculus on one side, *I love you* on the other. It was either from Winston or Hope.

Lacey called over to him. "Hey, Winston."

She watched playfully as he picked his head up out of the book and, half shaking, managed an awkward wave.

"Ummm . . . Hi, Lacey." He nervously put his book in his knapsack, got up, and started walking over to Lacey.

Lacey waved. "Hi, gorgeous." She blew him a sexy kiss and watched him freeze in his tracks.

"Ummm. Gotta go, Lacey. S-s-s-s-see you."

"See you around, cutie," Lacey said. But as his back

60

was turned to her, she stuck her fingers down her throat and made a gagging motion. "Blah."

"You're cold, Lacey. C-O-L-D," Renée said.

Penny laughed. "You're the funniest. Winston's probably going to the library to get a book on dos and don'ts on your first date."

"Well, his first date is over before it starts," Lacey swore. "Jess and Vaughn are the only ones I'm interested in around here. And Spike, except he doesn't seem to *be* around here. What about you guys? Where did Hal and Doug disappear to? I haven't seen either of them since assembly."

"Hal's whacking a tennis ball against the wall. That's all he ever does," Penny said, disgruntled. "He's got some big interstate tournament this weekend. Same old thing. They're always big tournaments to Hal. If he wins, we'll have a great weekend together. If he loses, the pits."

"He'll win," Lacey assured her. "How about Doug? I haven't seen you guys together much lately." Lacey turned to Renée and saw the long, sad look in her eyes.

Renée shrugged. "I don't know."

"Come on, Renée. What's up?" Lacey prodded.

Renée was slow to answer. She bit her lip and took a deep breath before confessing. "I think we're finished."

Lacey looked at Penny to find out if she knew

anything. But Penny's reaction told Lacey that it was news to her, too.

"What are you talking about?" Lacey asked. "Just last week you told me how great he was, helping you deal with April's murder. You said you wouldn't know what to do without him."

"I wouldn't," Renée answered. "But he doesn't care about me anymore. Not enough, anyway. It's been going on for a few weeks like this."

"Come on, out with it," Lacey insisted. "What happened? I thought you guys were solid."

"He's gonna leave me," Renée said. She was hyperventilating and tears suddenly began to stream down her cheeks. "He's decided to go to college in New York. Three thousand miles away. Like it doesn't matter what I want." She began to whimper. "You know what he said? 'We'll hang out on vacations and in the summer.' Hang out. Can you believe it? I thought he loved me. Now he just wants to hang out every time he happens to be in town."

"Wow. Sounds pretty serious," Penny remarked.

Lacey felt bad for her. Renée was shaking the way she did whenever she got too upset to cope.

Lacey placed a hand on Renée's shoulder. She pulled out the pink handkerchief and offered it to her. "Here. It's softer than Hagenspitzel's sleeve."

"Thanks, Lacey," Renée said with a little smile.

"You're incredible. You always know how to make me feel better."

"That's what I'm here for, babe," Lacey said.

Renée wiped her eyes. "I don't know. Maybe there's still hope. We're going out on Saturday night to try to patch things up. If I play my cards right, I think I can change his mind. I bought a real sexy dress yesterday. It's got black lace and it's cut real low in the back. Maybe you guys want to come help me pick out some shoes to match."

"Shhh. Renée, shut up," Penny warned.

Lacey shot Renée a nasty glare. Lacey's huge feet made it impossible for her to go to a shoe store without freaking out. Her friends usually knew better than to mention the subject in front of her.

"I'll go with you," Penny offered.

"Look, Renée," Lacey assured her, "by Saturday, you and Doug will be all patched up. I know it." Lacey saw a smile returning to Renée's face.

"So what are you and Hal gonna do this weekend?" Renée asked Penny.

"We were supposed to be going to the Madonna concert," Penny said. "Now, I don't know. Maybe we'll go bowling or something."

Laccy was sure that Penny had reminded her to make her feel bad for giving the tickets away to April instead of to Penny, as she had promised in the first place. Penny's expression told her that she was still brooding.

"I'm sorry, Pen." Lacey faked a super-guilty look. "I wish I had never given them to her. But you know . . . we can't do anything about it now."

Penny shrugged, but she had a testy expression on her face. "I know you did it for a good reason. You would have taken me otherwise. Right?"

"Sure, Penny." Lacey had given April the tickets in front of the whole school, hoping it would cast her in a good light right before the committee voted for Queen of the Peach Blossom Festival. She had offered them to Kiki too, so that she would drop out of the contest. Another botched plan. And even though Penny wasn't coming right out and saying it, it was obvious to Lacey that she was more than just upset.

"Hey, I've got a great idea!" Lacey exclaimed. "Let's have a party. I've got all Madonna's videos. We can hang out all night. You can sleep over again, Penny. It'll be a blast—our own private closed-circuit concert."

"Cool. But what about Hal?" Penny asked.

"What about him?" Lacey said, making it clear he was not invited.

"You're right. I'll blow him off. A special night for a couple of Pinks. He'll understand." Penny's eyes lit up. She raised her hand for a high-five from Lacey. "Just the two of us. I'm psyched."

"Me too, Pen. It'll be Madonna's loss not to have *us* there."

Lacey noticed that Renée's face was clouding over again. Following her friend's gaze, she saw Hal and Doug in the distance. Hal was wearing his tennis outfit and carrying a racket. Lacey pointed in their direction. "There are the lover boys now. Hey, beautiful!" she shouted.

"Lacey, shhh!" Renée gasped. She tried to hide behind Lacey and Penny.

"Relax, will you, babe?" Lacey said. "I just wanted to see which one would look."

"Oh, no, is he coming?" Renée panicked. "How do I look? Is my hair okay?"

"It's more than okay. You know I'd kill to have your hair," Penny said. "Besides, he's not even coming over. Look, I'm out of here. I'll see you guys later. Good luck with Doug." She waved good-bye as she got up and ran off to see Hal.

Lacey watched Penny go. "Man, she's impossible. So hyper."

"I think she gets mad that there's so much talk about April," Renée said. "I guess weird death reminds her of her baby sister. It hasn't really been very long since she died."

"Yeah, you're probably right." Lacey nodded. Lacey knew Penny still hadn't gotten over it. How could she, a baby sister dying in her crib? Lacey didn't know what could be worse. "Well, at least she manages to stay on top of things. Most of the time, anyway."

"You think I should go see Doug?" Renée asked, scared.

"Why not? What's there to be afraid of?" Lacey practically had to pick her up and force her to go. After a long hesitation, Renée finally got up.

"Okay," she promised. "One more try."

"Good luck, babe. Go get 'em." Lacey waved goodbye to Renée and then lay back down on the grass and closed her eyes.

All of a sudden an image of Winston Purdy III, madly pedaling his bicycle up Winding Hill Road, popped into Lacey's head. He was carrying a bouquet of roses, heavily in pursuit of her. Lacey got very depressed. At least there was one good thing about Winston, though. He was too nerdy to be a killer. Wasn't he?

No, Winston was definitely not April's murderer. The police report had said that April hadn't put up much of a fight. Even ultra-nice April Lovewell would have been able to fight off a geek like Winston Purdy. The killer was probably a real hunk with fabulous muscles, someone like Jess . . . or Vaughn. Now Vaughn Cutter, he was a real killer, all right. Tall, handsome, and dangerous, Lacey thought with a twinge of regret—regret that at that moment, killer

Vaughn was missing somewhere with Raven Cruz. Yeah, Lacey told herself with a little smile. Vaughn's Raven's killer now. Maybe Raven was going to get what she deserved for stealing Lacey's boyfriend after all.

CHAPTER 7

Kiki hung back from the door to the art room. Her head told her to go forward, but her legs didn't want to move. She could smell the turpentine and paint coming from the room—Mr. Woolery's cologne, some of the kids called it. Kiki could imagine him behind the door, his lean, muscular body in faded jeans, his movie-star-handsome face streaked with a stripe of red paint.

In her mind's eye, the paint turned into a splash of blood, as if someone had been trying to fight Mr. Woolery off. Last time she'd gone to see him outside of class time, it had been too weird. He'd had April's paintings spread out all over the floor, like an offering, and there was something in his intensity that had given Kiki the shivers. Or was it all in her mind?

Come on, Keeks, you're being silly, she chided herself. You've got a good idea for the April Foundation, and Mr. Woolery can help. Besides, what could he do to her in the middle of school, in the middle of the school day?

Mr. Woolery sat at his desk with his head down on his arms. From the doorway, Kiki cleared her throat. Mr. Woolery didn't budge. He was clearly lost in his own dark world. Were all the rumors around school getting to him? Or did he have some terrible secret to contemplate?

"Mr. Woolery?" Kiki said.

He jerked up his head. The startled expression on his weary face turned to a smile. "Kiki. Come in." Kiki entered the room slowly. Several easels were set up in different parts of the room. Behind Mr. Woolery's desk hung a small painting of trees in the scrubland at sunrise. Kiki recognized the long, loose brush strokes and striking colors. They were April's.

"I'm surprised you braved a visit," the art teacher said. "Folks around here are avoiding me like I was a guest from the underworld." He tried to make a joke of it, but Kiki could see sadness in his tired eyes.

Kiki gave a nervous laugh. "Well . . . I *am* here about April."

"Oh?" Mr. Woolery looked skittishly from Kiki to the door, and then back to Kiki again.

Kiki glanced over her shoulder. Two tenth-grade boys were walking by. "Yo, lady killer!" one of them yelled. They ran down the hall guffawing.

69

The corners of Mr. Woolery's mouth turned down. He got up from his desk, crossed the room, and closed the door. As it shut, Kiki felt the click of the latch echo in the pit of her stomach. Now it was just her and Mr. Woolery. Alone. Behind a closed door.

But she forced herself to go through with what she'd come to do. She heard her voice trembling. "Mr. Woolery, I'm here about the April Lovewell Memorial Foundation."

"Ah, yes." Mr. Woolery's face softened. "I think that's a wonderful idea. April was such a beautiful person—and her work was so beautiful."

Kiki felt her fear easing up. It seemed as if Mr. Woolery truly cared about April. "Now, how can I help your foundation?" he asked.

"Well, I was thinking about ways to raise money, and I remembered you saying you wanted to organize an exhibition of April's paintings and drawings."

Mr. Woolery shook his head. "I did want to. But now I don't think it's such a great idea."

"Why not?" Kiki asked, growing wary again.

Mr. Woolery began pacing the room. Kiki edged closer to the door. "I think," he said, "that people have linked my name with April's more than enough." He sounded hurt. And angry. "I think the best thing to do is to lay low, make myself as invisible as possible."

"But what about April?" Kiki said. She heard the

note of impatience in her voice. "Don't you want to do something for her?" Or was Mr. Woolery hiding something? Kiki watched him go back to his desk and sink into his chair.

"I'd like to help, Kiki, but I can't." Mr. Woolery picked up something off his desk and began to fiddle with it. A bracelet. A silver-and-turquoise bracelet. Raven's bracelet. Raven had been missing all day!

The walls were closing in around Kiki. Without even saying good-bye, she raced for the door and bolted from the room. She practically smacked right into Hope Hubbard. Stammering out an apology, Kiki glanced nervously at the art room door.

"Kiki, are you okay?" Hope followed her gaze.

Kiki managed a nod. Maybe it was all in her head.

But Hope lowered her voice and said confidentially, "I'm beginning to wonder about him."

"You too?" As the girls moved away from the art room door, Kiki told Hope about the bracelet.

"Oh, my God!" Hope said, her face creasing with fear and worry. "Look, Kiki, can you keep a secret?"

Kiki nodded. Paradiso was breeding secrets and rumors faster than a spy movie. "Do you know something about Woolery?"

"He's got an arrest record," Hope confided. She sounded relieved to be able to tell someone.

"He does? For what?"

71

"I don't know, but I'm going to find out," Hope said. "I only hope it's not too late for Raven."

Kiki looked back at the art room. She used to think Mr. Woolery was a total heartthrob. Now she wondered if looks could kill.

CHAPTER 8

Mademoiselle, Elle, Sassy, Seventeen . . . Every fashion magazine available was strewn about Lacey's bedroom. Lacey was in the middle of it all, sitting on the plush blue carpet, leaning against a cushioned footrest.

I'll be the hottest Peach Blossom Queen in Paradiso's history even if I have to go to Paris to find the right shoes, she vowed.

The sounds of KPOP and T.J. the D.J. had kept her entertained all afternoon. In honor of the upcoming Madonna concert, T.J. had been playing Madonna's albums back to back.

"And before we close out the Madonna special," T.J. the D.J. announced, "I'm going to give you all one more chance to win a pair of tix to Madonna's sold-out concert. This time we're gonna throw in a chauffeur-driven limo to take you to Sacramento in style. So get ready, cuz T.J. the D.J. is gonna take the very first caller. Starting . . ."

Lacey rushed to the phone and hit the speed button, already set for the station.

"NOW!"

Beep. Beep. Beep.

If I had known they were gonna offer tickets, I would have had Daddy hook up a special line to the station, she thought as she hung up the phone. Calvin Pinkerton had purchased KPOP with some other business partners a few months ago. Lacey felt cheated knowing that some kids, out of sheer luck, would see Madonna courtesy of her father, while two seats that once had been Lacey's would be empty the next evening. I was a fool for giving those tickets to April, she thought. If her parents found them, they probably burned them.

As angry as Lacey was, she couldn't help bopping to the tune. "Material Girl" was definitely her song. Lacey hummed to the music as she went back to work, searching for the right hairstyle.

Positive thoughts, Lacey, she told herself. I'm gonna be Peach Blossom Queen, I'm gonna have a gorgeous date for the ball, I'm gonna become a famous movie star, AND I'm definitely gonna find a great hairstyle.

Every few pages, she would tear out a picture and add it to a small but growing pile of possibilities.

Madonna's voice trailed off and T.J. the D.J. came back on. "Oh, Madonna, babe, I'll be seeing you tomorrow night. Can't wait. And neither can our lucky caller, Janice Campbell of Paradiso. That's what she just told me. Janice said she's taking her boyfriend, Jason Edwards, with her. Well, Jason, are you listening out there? See you guys tomorrow!"

I don't believe it. Janice and Jason? Give me a break. Lacey threw a magazine at one of the speakers, narrowly missing knocking it over.

The sounds of KPOP switched to Fifties oldies, which meant one thing—the Peach Blossom Festival. KPOP had been playing tons of them ever since the festival theme was announced.

The last notes of "Duke of Earl" were followed by the familiar sound of Buddy Holly. But as Buddy Holly sang, she heard a voice dubbed over it that was a lot more familiar than T.J. the D.J.'s. Coming through loud and clear was Calvin Pinkerton.

To the tune of "Peggy Sue," Daddy's pro-mall advertisement played. Lacey listened carefully.

"Pretty Peggy Sue. That's the way I like to think of dear, sweet April Lovewell. Only seventeen years old, and someone decided to take away the rest of her life. Just like that."

I thought *I* was his Pretty Peggy Sue. It was hard for Lacey to stomach.

"Hello, my name is Calvin Pinkerton. I knew April

Lovewell. My daughter, Lacey, was her classmate and her friend. We grieve about her death with the rest of the town of Paradiso. And throughout this time of sorrow, I contemplate how this tragedy might have been avoided. No, we can't bring April back. But we can keep this kind of horror from happening again in Paradiso."

Lacey was appalled. Everyone's going to make fun of Daddy. Just like after his ad in the *Record*. And they'll make fun of me too. I know it.

"I offer Paradiso my solution. A safe place for the children of our community to congregate. The Greenway Mall. Friends, I wonder, if April Lovewell had been in a secure, well-organized community setting on that fateful night, instead of walking the dark, empty streets of Paradiso, would she still be with us? Some of you feel that a mall is just a place to shop. The one that I propose to build promises to be a lot more than that. First and foremost, it will be a safe place. A healthy environment for people of all ages. For those of you who have expressed opposition to the Greenway Mall, I encourage you to contact my office so that we can discuss the project. I think I will be able to show you why Paradiso needs it. In honor of April Lovewell, Pretty Peggy Sue forever, I ask you all to think about it. Thank you."

Then T.J. the D.J.'s voice came through loud and clear. "I salute you, King Calvin," he said mockingly.

"My mall is your mall. Pardon me, sir. Your mall is my mall. Yessireee."

This was exactly the kind of thing Lacey was afraid of. She had grown up listening to T.J. He was like a close friend. How could he show such disrespect for her father—and his boss?

"Friends, I too grieve for April Lovewell. But the Greenway Mall? Maybe someone can explain to me exactly how a mall is gonna save a life. Give me a break, Pinkerton! I'm sorry, but T.J. the D.J. says NO WAY! Shame on you. Shame! This is the real world, Calvin. There's a murderer loose, and he doesn't give a hoot if there's a mall around or not. He wants to kill. And he just might be after Paradiso's next Peach Blossom winner. If I were you, Calvin, I'd be more worried about my own daughter than about a shopping mall."

"Shut up! SHUT UP!" Lacey rushed to the stereo and turned off the power. But the voice of T.J. continued. It was coming from downstairs!

I thought I was alone. Lacey walked over to her bedroom door and opened it. She could make out the sound of her father's voice, ranting and raving over T.J.'s comments. She tiptoed to the top of the stairs and crouched down. Her mother was there too. Lacey held on tightly to the banister and listened.

T.J. the D.J. had gotten completely wrapped up in his attack on Calvin, making harsh statements about the Pinkerton wealth and power. He laid into the whole family, calling Darla a silent partner in Calvin's vicious, criminal pursuit of control over Paradiso. And he called Lacey the beautiful princess who was learning the evil ways of her family so that she, too, could one day rule with an iron fist.

T.J. wouldn't stop. ". . . I was born here. I remember the days when this was the sweetest, simplest town in the whole damn state. Paradiso *was* paradise to me. Then came the canneries. And with that, the controversy over the migrant farmers. How many of us know someone who was fired by Calvin Pinkerton? How many know how hard it is to pay the rent with the two bits King Calvin pays you? How many of us write his name, in some way or another, every time we pay a rent check? Or a grocery bill? It's time to put our feet down and just say no!"

Lacey listened in horror. She looked at her father, fuming with rage. He was home so early in the day. And he was drinking. Earlier and earlier every day. Darla sat there, stewing, a drink in her hand too.

Please stop, T.J., please! Lacey pleaded silently. Finally, he ended his assault and the mellow sound of Nat King Cole filled the Pinkerton house. It was a strange accompaniment to the wild roar of Calvin Pinkerton.

"That little worm! I don't think our little T.J. the D.J. understands just who I am. Well, he will," Calvin

Pinkerton raved, just before he polished off the remains of his drink. "Where's that bottle," he mumbled. He grabbed the bottle from the side table next to the stereo. "Damn you!" he screamed at the speaker. "Blasted idiot. Who do you think you're talking to, anyway? Don't ever play games with me."

Lacey had seen her father every kind of angry, but this was the worst ever. She shuddered as she watched him kick the speaker over. He picked up an antique Chinese vase and hurled it against the fireplace. It probably cost more money than most of Lacey's friends' parents would make in a year.

"Calvin, no," Darla begged.

He took a big gulp from the bottle of whiskey and fell to his knees. "They're going to ruin me. The whole damn town is gunning for me."

Please, Daddy. Please stop. Lacey was helpless. She prayed it would end.

"We're losing control of this town, Calvin," her mother said. "And all you can do is whine."

"No! I'm going to fix everything. I will!" Calvin sounded pathetic.

"And how do you propose to do that? Hmmm. What's King Calvin going to do next? You said April's death would solve everything. The mall for you and the crown for Lacey. If that dreadful disc jockey is any indication, you've failed."

Lacey's mouth hung wide open. Failed? At what? What had they done?

Darla swallowed a huge gulp of vodka and continued. "And that Cruz girl. That Raven Cruz. You couldn't even handle that one. You were supposed to take care of her, Calvin. How can that little nothing stop our mall?"

"I will, I will. I'll fix her. Believe me. I just need time."

Lacey knew she should get away; there would be hell to pay if her parents saw her there. But she sat, transfixed.

"Time? We have plenty of that now, don't we? Senator Miller and his damn filibuster have given us all the time in the world. And it's costing us millions waiting while the work on the mall is held up." Darla took another swig and refilled her glass. "Don't forget that fifty percent of Pinkerton Enterprises is mine, and I don't want to see it go bust. Do something and do it fast."

Do something? What are they up to? What did they do to April? To Raven? Lacey was afraid to admit to herself what she was thinking. *Murder?* She closed her eyes and pressed her hands to her head, as if she might squeeze out the horrible thoughts.

Lacey watched as Darla reached for the phone. "Bring the car up front immediately, Manuel." She got up and went to the front hall. Lacey silently moved down a step to watch. Darla stood before the hall mirror. She shook her head in disgust. "Miserable life. A miserable life in a miserable place." She grabbed her bag from the side table next to her and took out her dark sunglasses. She shot one more glare at Calvin, who was stumbling around the living room. Then she opened the door and staggered out.

Lacey's body shook with silent tears. She had never been so scared. Could the welts on the backs of her legs be just a small sign of what Calvin was really all about? And Darla. Now she was talking about Raven. Raven, who was missing. And there was Darla's mysterious run-in with Kiki. Had she had one with April too? Lacey thought she might throw up.

"Lacey!" Calvin Pinkerton thundered.

Oh, my God! Lacey panicked as their eyes met in the glass.

Calvin let the bottle drop to the ground and stumbled to the foot of the stairs. "What are you doing up there?"

"Daddy. I'm sorry. I'm sorry," was all she could manage.

"So now my little princess is spying on her daddy?"

"No." Lacey backed up, one step at a time, praying he wouldn't follow.

"Come here, at once. We're going to have ourselves a little talk, princess." He was totally insane.

"Please. No." She continued to back away, but he followed, tripping as he made his way up the stairs.

Lacey ran to the bathroom and shut the door. Her hands shook uncontrollably as she tried to turn the lock. It was no use. Before she could fasten the latch, Calvin threw the door open and thundered in, his face twisted by rage and whiskey.

CHAPTER 9

The prison loomed over the landscape, a heavy, dark, armored building. Hope and Jess drove into its shadow, and Hope went cold all over. It was so bleak. If April's killer were in there, I wouldn't be half as afraid, Hope thought.

Jess followed signs to the visitors' parking lot and pulled into a space. He shut off the motor, but neither he nor Hope moved. "You don't want to go in there either, huh?" he asked.

Hope shook her head. "It kind of makes you wonder what Spike's father did to get put in a place like this." She didn't add anything, but she knew they were both thinking the same thing. Was it murder? Like father, like son?

"Well, whatever it was, he can't hurt us behind bars. And we might find out something to help us find Spike," Jess said. He got out of the car, and Hope followed him. Hand in hand, they approached the entrance to Merryville State Prison. As Hope crossed the threshold and left the afternoon light behind, every muscle in her body contracted.

Inside the prison, Hope and Jess were sent directly to the deputy warden's office because they didn't know Mr. Navarrone's first name or cell number.

"Kind of like getting sent to the Dweeb," Jess tried to joke, their footsteps echoing down the concrete hall to the office.

When she saw the man behind the desk, Hope's nervous laugh froze in her throat. He had the build of a heavyweight fighter, and his deeply pockmarked face was set in a frightening scowl.

"Yes?" he snarled. It sounded like an accusation.

"We, um, we're looking for our friend's father," Hope stammered. "They told us you could look up his cell number." Hope prayed he hadn't heard the bulletin out for Spike. He looked as if he might be happy to lock them up just for knowing a suspected criminal.

He stood up from his desk, his stomach straining the belt of his uniform, and lumbered over to a computer against the wall. "Navarrone. Navarrone," he mumbled irritably. He started tapping at the keyboard.

Suddenly, a tingle ran up Hope's spine. What if Mr. Woolery's conviction record was somewhere in the files that the deputy warden was punching into?

Hope sidled closer to the computer and positioned herself so that if she craned her neck, she could get a look at the screen. She held her breath, praying that he wouldn't notice.

His gaze was fastened on the screen and a string of seemingly unrelated numbers and letters. It was an access code Hope never would have been able to guess at in a million years. She repeated it to herself several times. But it was complicated. She didn't trust herself to remember it.

"Ah, warden, is there a ladies' room here?" she asked, silently chanting the access code to keep it in her head.

He looked as if the interruption were a federal crime. He glared at her, and pointed a thick finger at a door at the other end of the room.

Hope repeated the numbers and letters to herself as she went into the bathroom and locked the door. But she didn't have anything to write with. She thought fast. She pulled off a few sheets of toilet paper. Then she ran her index finger over her lips. A trace of pinky red came off on her fingertip. There would have been more if she and Jess hadn't kissed at a red light on the way.

She drew her finger across the toilet tissue and made a *W*. It was faint and blurry, and the paper pulled and threatened to rip, but the lip gloss left enough of a trace to make it out later. Working quickly and carefully, she wrote down the rest of the code. She folded the toilet paper and put it in the back pocket of her jeans. Then she reconsidered. Did they search you when you went to visit a prisoner? Stealing this access code was probably a *real* federal crime—and she was committing it right under the barbed-wire roof of Merryville Prison. She tucked the piece of paper into her sock, easing it down under the arch of her foot. She flushed the toilet and came back out to the warden's office.

"Carlos!" Jess announced.

"Huh?" Hope was thinking about the damaging evidence inside her shoe.

"Spike's dad's name is Carlos Navarrone," Jess said.

Like father, like son, Hope couldn't help thinking again.

They followed the deputy warden's directions to a room that was divided by a transparent plastic wall. The wall was lined with little booths, like computer stations. Each booth faced an identical booth on the other side of the wall. And in each booth was a telephone to talk to the inmate on the other side. A man in a dark suit fought heatedly over the phone with the prisoner facing him through the wall. A mother and her two little girls visited with their husband and father. An old woman visited with a young man. Her son?

It was just like the movies.

Hope and Jess were shown to an empty booth. A few moments later, Mr. Navarrone was led in. Hope would have recognized him anywhere. He was handsome, with dark eyes and skin and thick dark hair. He was young—he looked just like Spike. He sat down opposite them, giving them a curious though not unfriendly look. He picked up the phone.

Jess looked at Hope. "You want to do the talking?"

Hope picked up the phone on their side of the wall. "Hi, Mr. Navarrone," she said. She felt awfully strange talking to someone who was only a few feet away by phone. "My name's Hope Hubbard. And this is Jess Gardner. We're friends of Spike's." Or *were* friends, she thought.

Mr. Navarrone's face lit up. "Then I'm pleased to meet you." He seemed so genuine.

Hope felt bad about her doubts about Spike. And about the news that she had to give Mr. Navarrone. She took a breath. "Mr. Navarrone, Spike—well, he's left Paradiso," she said.

Through the Plexiglas partition, Mr. Navarrone didn't register a bit of surprise. He just nodded and said, "I know. And you want to know if I know where he is. You're not the first visitors I've gotten."

"Sheriff Rodriguez?" Hope asked.

"Yes. And a lady reporter. Willa something." Willa Flicker! So she'd been around asking questions too.

"I'll tell you what I told them," Spike's dad went on. "I don't know where Carlos is."

He shook his head and sighed. "It's not like Carlos. Not like him at all, to leave his brothers like that. He loves those two little guys . . . as much as I do."

Hope nodded. "But he did leave."

Mr. Navarrone sighed into the telephone receiver again. "He should have known better," he said, more to himself than to Hope.

"He should have? Why?" she asked.

Mr. Navarrone frowned. "Well . . . he saw the trouble it caused when I ran away."

"You did?" She was almost afraid to find out why.

"I'm not going to tell you I was an angel or anything," Mr. Navarrone said. "I was an accomplice to a robbery at the canneries. I told myself, if they wouldn't pay a fair wage, I was entitled to take what I could get. I drove the getaway car. My job was to sit outside in the van. Well, the job got bungled, and I wound up taking the heat. So I took off. I committed the crime to take care of my family, but I wound up leaving them in the lurch." He swallowed hard, and his voice got softer. "If Spike's mama drinks, it's my fault." He shook his head. "Running away never helps anything."

Hope heard Mr. Navarrone echoing her own sentiments, and she thought of her own father. She'd been so young when he left that she couldn't even remember him. "I agree with you," Hope said. "I tried to convince Spike not to go. . . . But I guess he got scared." *Either that, or he's guilty.*

Mr. Navarrone's mouth turned down and frown lines appeared deep in his face. "He shouldn't be scared of the truth. And I'm sure the truth is that my son didn't do anything wrong."

Hope wanted to agree, but she thought of the size 10½ footprint. She didn't say anything.

Behind the partition, Mr. Navarrone's face seemed to sag. "Last time Spike came to see me, he was so happy. I think it was the girl—April."

Hope felt an ache deep inside at the mention of her cousin.

"He told me about how they'd meet under a ponderosa pine, a special place that was just theirs."

Hope sat straight up. The spot in April's note! Pay dirt! Except that ponderosa pines were a dime a dozen in Paradiso. The special spot could be almost anywhere. "Mr. Navarrone, you don't know where exactly that place was, do you?"

Mr. Navarrone shook his head. "Only that they used to go there and dream about how they were going to get out of Paradiso and make a life in a new place. Spike told me, 'Dad, April's going to be someone—maybe even a famous artist. She's not going to stick around Paradiso with nothing to do but wait for the peach trees to blossom.' I think April was Spike's ticket out of here."

Hope bit her lip. Ultimately, April *had* been Spike's reason for leaving Paradiso. But not in the way anyone had thought. Hope couldn't fight back the ugly idea forming in her head. April's pregnancy would have put an end to her and Spike's dreams. How badly had Spike wanted to get out of Paradiso? Bad enough to kill?

"Mr. Navarrone, people are saying that Spike practically confessed to the murder by taking off," Hope suggested, her fears about Spike growing.

Mr. Navarrone shook his head hard. "No way. My son cared for April. He wouldn't have harmed her for anything in the world. Her, or anyone else. But he's got to come back." Mr. Navarrone hung his head. "Otherwise, he doesn't stand a chance. I was born in this country, and so was Spike, but people see us and they think Mexican. Alien. Trouble. A Mexican running from the law, well . . ."

Hope knew that Mr. Navarrone was right about that much.

"The only way out is to give himself up on his own. Before the police find him," Mr. Navarrone said. "If my son is a man, he'll face the charges. And he'll prove them wrong. I—I don't want him to end up like me. . . ."

"Well, we'd like to help you find him," Hope said.

"Promise me you will," Mr. Navarrone pleaded, his dark eyes flashing urgently.

"We'll do our best," Hope said. She had her own reasons to find him too.

Mr. Navarrone thanked her for the visit. "It's a pleasure to meet two of my son's friends. When I get out, I want to know them all. When I get out. . . ." He gave a bittersweet smile.

Hope and Jess said good-bye. Mr. Navarrone hung up the telephone and stood. He pressed his hand to the panel that separated them, in a hopeless effort to touch, to make human contact.

Hope pressed her hand to the plastic opposite Mr. Navarrone's hand. It was cold and hard.

As they watched Mr. Navarrone turn away in his prison uniform, Hope shuddered. She looked at Jess and could tell he was thinking the same thing: Mr. Navarrone looked exactly like Spike from the back. Like father, like son. Hope took Jess's hand, and they walked out of the now empty room. "I wonder if we'll be visiting Spike here someday," Hope said.

Jess frowned and glanced back. "It may be someday soon."

CHAPTER 10

Raven was dancing in her seat to the music pouring out of Vaughn's car radio. Her bracelets jingled in rhythm. "They're playing our song, Vaughn. How did T.J. the D.J. know?"

"Maybe he could feel our good vibes all the way from the cabin," Vaughn joked. "Maybe he picked them up like radio waves." He reached out and let his hand rest on Raven's leg as the song ended and a voice announced, "You just heard the Everly Brothers' 'Wake Up Little Susie' at six-fifteen on a SPECTAC-ULAR sunny Paradiso afternoon. This is KPOP ra-dio . . ."

Raven covered Vaughn's hand with her own. Deep inside, a little voice was saying "Guilty, guilty, guilty." Raven had never stayed out all night before—even if it hadn't been on purpose. They'd just fallen asleep. She knew Papa and Mama would be terribly worried.

But it was such a sunny, beautiful day out, and she was with the hottest guy in Paradiso.

They'd spent the morning eating breakfast in a little inn Vaughn knew of by the lake, and later they'd braved the springtime water for a brisk swim and lain out on some warm rocks to bask in the sun. Those memories—and the ones from the night before—shimmered around Raven like sunlight on leaves.

Last night. Last night had been part fantasy, part nightmare. Things between Raven and Vaughn had been going great; then, suddenly, Vaughn had totally lost control. For a few minutes, Raven was actually scared—no, terrified—that he might hurt her. What still scared her was her realization that Vaughn must have been frightened of the same thing—so frightened that he had stormed off to be alone until he was in control again.

But then he had returned to her—taking her in his arms in front of the fire and holding her, so tender, so apologetic, that her fear and doubt had just melted away.

As Vaughn drove past the green and white sign that announced ENTERING PARADISO, ESTABLISHED 1919, the little voice in Raven's head grew louder. GUILTY! True, there was no telephone in the Cutter cabin, but she should have gotten Vaughn to drive her to the nearest pay phone the instant they'd found themselves waking up to the light of a new day.

Especially with Mama sick. The problem was, Raven hadn't wanted to face Papa's anger. But there was no more putting it off. She could hear him now: "Your mother and I have been worried to death!" Raven crossed her fingers and prayed that it wouldn't be too, too awful.

"Vaughn, aren't you scared about what your parents are going to say?"

Vaughn raised his muscular shoulders. "Them? I'd be surprised if they noticed I was gone. It's been so bad with them lately that I'm outta there as soon as I wake up. They probably just think that I was out late and left early."

Vaughn turned onto the road that led out to Rosa's Café. As she got closer to home, Raven felt all her problems edging their way past the warm feelings of last night and the leisurely, sun-kissed morning she and Vaughn had shared. In addition to the worries about what her parents were going to say, there was the fight to save the scrublands, and Cal Pinkerton's bribe, and how she was going to pay for college without accepting Pinkerton's money.

"Vaughn?" she said.

"Yeah?" Vaughn had a big smile on his strong-boned, handsome face. The shadows over Paradiso hadn't caught up to him yet.

"Vaughn, you wouldn't take money to do something against your principles, would you?" Raven asked, thinking about the one hundred dollars Lacey's father had handed her, now tucked away under the bill drawer of the cash register at Rosa's.

"Why? You going to pay me to kidnap you to the cabin for the rest of the year?"

Raven laughed. "I said against your principles. I like to think you'd be totally happy to kidnap me to the cabin—for free." She leaned over and gave him a kiss on the cheek.

"If that's the payment, I might be tempted . . ."

Raven grew serious again. "No, really, Vaughn."

"Do something I didn't want to do for money? No way," Vaughn answered just as seriously. "That'd be as bad as my dad and Cal Pinkerton. Totally low down. What are you talking about, Raven?"

"I don't know . . . I was just thinking." Raven let the subject drop.

Another song ended on the radio, and a voice came through the car speakers. "This is Temporary Tom, filling in for T.J. the D.J.," he said.

Raven knit her brow. "Hey, what happened to T.J.?"

Temporary Tom didn't offer a clue. "In Paradiso," he said, "the search continues for the killer of April Lovewell." Raven felt her mouth turn down. The cabin was beginning to seem a world away.

"The police have put out a statewide APB for Carlos Navarrone, better known as Spike, who is believed to have been Miss Lovewell's boyfriend and who is now wanted for questioning about her murder," the D.J. went on.

Vaughn's easy smile had faded too. "Wow! Spike's gone? And they're looking for him?" He shook his head. "Bad news, man." He steered the Jag past the edge of the scrublands, which spread out in the afternoon sun. A coal-black bird, riding the breeze like a glider, let out a menacing caw.

"On a happier note," said Temporary Tom, "the Paradiso Peach Blossom Festival has been rescheduled for the weekend after this one, so get your saddle shoes and poodle skirts ready, gals, and get out those letter sweaters, guys! Our Queen will be one of three lovely students at Paradiso High: Miss Lacey Pinkerton, Miss Kiki De Santis, and Miss Raven Cruz."

"The loveliest of the lovelies," Vaughn added.

Raven was about to reward Vaughn with an appropriately grateful kiss when she saw the flashing red lights. An ambulance was parked next to the Cruzes' truck in the parking lot of Rosa's Café.

Raven bolted from the car before Vaughn had even pulled to a complete stop. She ran around the back of the café to where she and her family lived, pushing open the front door and racing inside. "Mama! Mama!" she screamed. Her breath came fast and shallow.

She ran right into Papa's arms. "Raven! My God,

you're all right," he said in Spanish. "Thank heavens." He took a step back. "Where have you been? What happened?"

The ambulance driver and another attendant came out of her parents' room. "Mama!" Raven said again.

"She's in bed," Papa said.

"Is she—all right?" Raven looked at her father, then at the men from the hospital.

"She took a turn for the worse," Papa said, and Raven could hear his voice shaking. "You can go," he said to the two men.

"But she's home," Raven said as the men from the hospital left. "They brought her home. She must be better."

Papa shook his head.

"Then why did they bring her back here?" Raven's voice rose to the beams of the small house.

It took Papa a long while to answer. "No medical insurance," he finally said. "We couldn't afford to keep her in there, so they brought her back."

Raven felt her pulse racing hysterically. "They brought her back? To die! Papa, she's sick! She needs medical attention!" Raven struggled from his grasp and headed for the bedroom. "I have to see her! Mama!"

Papa grabbed her arm and stopped her. "Raven, lower your voice. She's asleep. I don't want you disturbing her. She's not going to die." But he didn't sound very convinced himself.

Vaughn appeared in the doorway and knocked softly on the open door before coming in. Papa looked from him to Raven and back to him. "Is this why you didn't come home last night? Why you worried your mother and me so much that . . . that . . ." he sputtered.

Raven hung her head in shame. Mama was sick, maybe dying, and it was partly her fault. She could feel Papa standing over her, his presence dark and angry, waiting for an explanation.

"I'm sorry, Papa," she whispered. Tears were already gathering behind her eyelids. "I didn't mean to stay out. We—we fell asleep." Her cheeks were hot.

"You fell asleep? With Vaughn?"

Raven saw Vaughn give a start as he recognized his own name in Mr. Cruz's rapid-fire stream of Spanish.

"Maybe I should explain . . ." he said, taking a step forward.

"Vaughn, I think it would be best if I talked to my daughter alone," Mr. Cruz answered in English.

Vaughn nodded and left. Through the small living room window, Raven watched him go and felt the burn of tears in her eyes. Shopping malls, bribes, murder, pain, and now, trouble and unhappiness where there should have been only joy and love. Maybe

Paradiso was a town under a curse. Maybe Spike could see it, and that was why he had left. Maybe Raven and Vaughn should have left Paradiso and stayed away forever, too.

CHAPTER 11

Kiki opened her door to find Vaughn on the front porch. "Vaughn! Thank goodness you're all right!" She threw her arms around him and gave him a sisterly hug. He was tense and unresponsive. She stepped back. "But you're not all right," she said. Vaughn looked terrible, his face drawn, his jaw tight. "What? What happened? Where's Raven?"

"She's at home."

"Oh." Kiki relaxed a little. "Then what? You want to come in?"

Vaughn peered behind her. "Are your folks around? I kind of need to talk in private."

"They're in the dining room having dessert," Kiki said. "We can go sit by the pool, if you want. No one'll bother us out there."

Vaughn nodded. "Thanks."

"Mom? Dad?" she called. "I'll be by the pool with Vaughn, okay?"

"Okay, sweetie. Does Vaughn want a piece of chocolate cake?" her mother called back.

"No, thanks, Mrs. De Santis. I don't think I could eat anything."

"That bad?" Kiki asked.

Vaughn sighed. "The roof just blew off at home," he said. Kiki automatically looked toward the Cutter estate. "I don't mean literally," Vaughn said, managing a little laugh. "I mean about SCAM and Raven and everything."

Kiki led the way around the dark, shimmering pool and unfolded two plastic lounge chairs next to it. She stretched out on one of them and looked up, but there weren't any stars. "Where were you guys today, anyway? Everyone was scared to death about you," Kiki said. "Me included." She was so relieved that her friends were safe.

Vaughn eased his bulky frame into his chair. "Hey, I'm sorry. We went up to the cabin, and, well, one thing led to another and . . ."

"And you didn't come back until today," Kiki finished. "Boy, I'd expect to see a much happier look on your face from the sound of things, Vaughn Cutter."

But Vaughn didn't crack a smile.

"Uh-oh. Your parents were furious?"

Vaughn nodded. "I figured they probably wouldn't

even know I'd been gone. But they were waiting for me when I got home. Sitting there, all stiff and proper in the living room—they never go in there unless it's some kind of formal occasion."

"They knew?"

"Yeah," Vaughn said. "I guess Mr. Cruz called the school to find Raven, and then Appleby called my folks. They knew that I'd been out all night, and they knew who I'd been with."

"So they know about you and Raven now," Kiki said. "So."

"Yeah, and they want me to break up with her. No, not want—they ordered me to. My dad accused me of being in SCAM just because of Raven. They said I never would have gotten involved if it wasn't for her."

"Did you tell them it wasn't true?" Kiki asked.

"I tried to. But they'd already tried me and found me guilty before I'd even walked in the door." Vaughn's voice cracked with anger.

"Well, there's no way they can force you to stop seeing each other," she said, trying to soothe his rising temper.

"Oh, yeah?"

Kiki sat up and looked at Vaughn. His fists were clenched. "Vaughn," she said softly, "Hope and April were best friends even though their parents disapproved of their friendship for seventeen years. If you want to be with Raven, you'll find a way. What are they gonna do? Lock you in your room and never let you out?"

"Worse. They're going to take my room away completely! They said they'd disinherit me."

Kiki couldn't believe what she'd heard. "You mean, like cut you out of their will?"

Vaughn ran a hand through his hair. "And out of their house and out of their lives. You know what it means to disinherit someone? It's like saying that they're dead. That they've never been born."

Kiki looked through the back window to where her parents sat in the dining room. With the room lit up, she could see them talking—and smiling at each other. Her mother and father might not be glamorous and important and fabulously wealthy, but she wouldn't trade them for all of the Cutters' millions. Or the Pinkertons' billions.

"So what are you going to do?" Kiki asked.

"I don't know. It's either give up Raven and quit SCAM, or find myself a tent and pitch it behind school." It was too dark to see Vaughn's face very clearly, but Kiki could hear his words coming out through a clenched jaw. "I think I could reason with Mom if Dad weren't around, but he's a damned rock."

"Vaughn, you've got to figure out some way of living with them and making peace," Kiki said. "They *are* your parents."

"That's the worst part," Vaughn said. The anger in his voice was building toward a breaking point. Kiki automatically stiffened.

"I wish I could give you some advice," she said. A dog howled low and long in the distance.

"Advice? What I need is a new set of parents, damn them!" Vaughn pounded at the lounge chair. Suddenly, it gave way beneath him. Vaughn grabbed the chair and hurled it into the pool. It slashed the water's surface.

Kiki gasped. Then it was silent, except for the ripples of water lapping against the side of the pool. A section of the chair's metal frame poked up from a corner of the shallow end.

"Look, I'm sorry," Vaughn finally said. He went over and fished out the chair. He set it down, dripping, near the edge of the pool. "I'm sorry, Kiki."

"It's okay," Kiki managed weakly.

"Maybe I should go," Vaughn said. "Thanks for listening."

"Vaughn, just try to take it easy, okay?" Kiki said. But she knew her words were lost on him. She watched him cross the back lawn, his shoulders slumped and his strides heavy.

When he was gone, Kiki let herself in the back door and went into the dining room. She threw her arms around each of her parents in turn.

"Hey, Weets," her father said, using her old nickname. "What's that for?"

Kiki shrugged. "Just because."

"Honey," her mother said, "we love you too."

It was a sentiment that seemed to be missing in Paradiso lately.

CHAPTER 12

Hope typed in the secret code she'd copied down in the deputy warden's office at the prison. She pushed the enter key and held her breath. Work. Please work, she pleaded silently.

Her computer hummed softly. In rapid sequence the most incredible words appeared on the screen. STATE OF CALIFORNIA, CLASSIFIED INFORMATION. Hope let out a cheer and raised her right fist in the air. This was it! This was the key that would unlock Mark Woolery's secret!

She worked the keyboard for a few minutes until she discovered the part of the file she wanted. Finally, she got the prompt she'd been searching for ever since she'd seen Mr. Woolery's school file in the computer. LAST NAME, FIRST NAME.

WOOLERY, she typed. What was that outside? Hope raced over and looked out the open window. Nothing.

No one. "Who's there?" she called into the thick, dark night. Her only answer was the rustling of leaves. She went back to her machine. MARK. She glanced at the window, but saw only the reflection from her desk lamp in the top pane, like the sun at the top corner of a child's drawing. She hit the enter key . . .

. . . And Mr. Woolery's secret unfolded in front of her eyes.

STATE OF CALIFORNIA DIVISION OF CRIMINAL JUSTICE SERVICES read the top of her computer screen. CONFIDENTIAL TO SACRAMENTO POLICE HEADQUARTERS. NAME: MARK P. WOOLERY. DATE OF BIRTH, RACE, SEX, HEIGHT, SOCIAL SECURITY NUMBER. Hope skimmed the information. OTHER NAMES USED BY SUBJECT. That one was blank. CRIMINAL HISTORY. Also blank. ARREST INFORMATION. This was what Hope was looking for. DATE. Hope did some quick arithmetic. Mr. Woolery had been arrested five years ago, almost to the day. PLACE. MORRISTOWN NUCLEAR POWER PLANT, NEW YORK STATE.

Mr. Woolery had been arrested at a nuclear plant? ARREST ARRAIGNMENT CHARGES. CRIMINAL TRESPASS AND CRIMINAL MISCHIEF. DISPOSITION. CRIMINAL TRESPASS AND HOLDING A DEMONSTRATION WITHOUT A LICENSE.

Criminal trespass! Mr. Woolery wasn't a murderer. He'd been demonstrating against a nuclear power station. Hope had a moment of relief, followed by a new worry. If Mr. Woolery turned out to be innocent, there was even more reason to suspect that Spike Navarrone was guilty. *Somebody* had killed April Lovewell.

Since April's death, it seemed as if good news was only the prelude to bad. Just a short while ago, Jess had called with the welcome message that Vaughn and Raven were home and safe. Then he'd told her the rest of it: Raven's mother was sick, and Vaughn's parents had declared war on their own son.

Where will it end? Hope wondered as she picked up the phone to call Kiki. She felt so confused. She was glad Mr. Woolery wasn't a criminal. But there was no resting easy until April's killer was found.

"Hello?" Kiki's voice came over the line.

"Kiki? Hope."

"Hope, hi! Did you find out something about Woolery?"

"Yeah. He's guilty. But he's innocent." She laughed and told Kiki what she'd discovered.

"Oh, wow! What a relief!" Kiki said.

"Yeah," Hope agreed. "We were getting suspicious of the wrong person. At least I think we were."

"Oh, that's so great!" Kiki said. She giggled. "Hey, now we can all go back to having a huge crush on him!" Then her laughter stopped. "But if it's not him . . ."

Hope blew out a long breath. "Yeah, that's exactly how I feel. Kiki, I have this awful idea."

"Yeah?" Kiki asked, sounding nervous now.

"What if we made an innocent person out to be guilty, but we made a guilty person out to be innocent?" Hope said. "Because he's our friend."

There was a long silence over the phone. Then Kiki said, "Spike?" From her tone of voice, Hope could picture her shaking her long brown hair. "But he's such a cool guy. I—I always thought April was pretty lucky to be going out with him."

"Maybe not so lucky." Hope hated herself for thinking this way about Spike. April had loved him. "If I could find the place where he and April were supposed to meet the night she was killed, maybe I'd find some clue," Hope added, almost to herself.

In the silence from Kiki's end, Hope was sure she heard a noise outside her window again. Yes, a soft cracking sound, as if someone had stepped on a twig. Hubbard, you're giving yourself a case of the spooks, she scolded herself silently.

Kiki's voice came over the line again. "I don't know, Hope," she finally said. "The killer could be anyone. I got a visit from Lacey's mom, and she did everything but tell me I was going to be the next murder victim if I didn't drop out of the contest for Peggy Sue."

Hope whistled. "She did? Well, Lacey's father's

making the most out of April's death too. Did you see that ad in the *Record*?"

"Yeah, it was pretty slimy," Kiki said. "And did you hear he got T.J. the D.J. fired for saying so?"

"Wow! Is that what happened?" Hope asked. "Kiki, do you suppose that if Lacey's dad got rid of T.J. so easily, maybe he got rid of April too?"

"For the mall," Kiki hypothesized.

"Or for Lacey, so his princess could be Queen." Suddenly Hope remembered that she was talking to Lacey's best friend—even though everyone at school knew they were in the middle of a huge fight. "I'm sorry, Kiki. I take that back."

"No, it's okay," Kiki said slowly. "I thought I knew her so well, but maybe I don't. Maybe I don't know anyone that well."

"Look, Kiki, you know Lacey Pinkerton better than almost anyone. The thing is, we're all scared." Hope glanced at her window once more.

"You can say that again," Kiki agreed. "Well, at least Mr. Woolery's someone we don't have to be scared of anymore. I think." But she didn't even sound certain of that. "I guess I should go and talk to him about putting on that exhibition of April's art again."

"April would have liked that," Hope said. "She always used to say stuff like, 'When I have my first

110

show . . .' " Hope felt an unexpected rush of silent tears.

"You must miss her so much," Kiki said quietly.

"Yeah." The word came out hoarse.

"Well, you can call me whenever you want," Kiki offered. "You know that."

"Thanks, Kiki. See you in school, okay?"

"Okay. Bye, Hope. Thanks for calling."

Hope hung up the phone. Kiki De Santis was as nice as everyone said she was. But no one could replace April. It had been two weeks. And they weren't any closer to finding the killer than they had been the day after the murder.

Hope went over to her window. She shut and locked it.

CHAPTER 13

CRASH! The plate of *huevos rancheros* shattered at Raven's feet. Blood-red salsa sprayed up and splattered her white waitress uniform. At the corner table, a harried group of salesmen were yelling for the check. Two more orders were lined up on the ledge between the kitchen and the counter area.

"Order's up!" Papa called. He stuck his head through the little window and shot Raven a dark look. He had never been this angry at her before. "Don't you hear me ringing the bell to pick up the food?"

Raven felt as if she were about to break, just as easily as the plate at her feet. She was so worried about Mama. And she felt so guilty. *Maybe if I hadn't gotten her so upset, she wouldn't have had to go to the hospital in the first place.*

She ran over and grabbed the two orders, balancing several plates on her arm. Where was Papa going to get the money to pay for all of Mama's medical bills? The doctors still weren't sure what she had, and all the tests they wanted to give her were so expensive.

Raven made a wide circle around the spilled eggs to serve her orders. Then she whisked out her order pad and began adding up the corner table's check.

"Miss? Um, miss? Some more coffee, please?"

"Just a moment," Raven said. She made a mental note. Coffee at table two. Then she'd clean up that mess in the middle of the floor. Oh, and she had to put in a new order for those spilled eggs. On the double.

She tried to work in an orderly, organized way. But she was lost in thoughts of Mama, and it was hard to concentrate on what she was doing. The big red-haired man at the corner table got up and lumbered over to the cash register. Raven rushed over. As she rang up his check, the cash drawer sprang open with a sharp *ping!* She thought of Calvin Pinkerton's money, nestled under the bill drawer. If he was willing to pay for college, he might be willing to pay for Mama's medical expenses.

But at what cost? Outside the windows on one side of the café, the scrublands seemed to be a magnet for the hazy, early morning light.

"My change, miss?" the red-haired man asked.

"Oops, I'm sorry." Raven counted it out to him.

She still hadn't brought table two their coffee or cleaned up the mess.

The bell over the door to the café signaled another customer. Raven looked to the entrance, wishing whoever it was would decide to go away. But it was Vaughn who came through the door, and Raven's mood picked up. She raced over to him and stood on tiptoe to stretch up and give him a kiss.

"Bad morning?" Vaughn glanced at the broken plate on the floor.

Raven let out a sigh of frustration. "Papa's furious. Mama's sick. I'm trying to do everything at once." All the pressures came rushing out. "At lunch I've got to figure out a way to come back here and take care of Mama and chair the SCAM meeting at the same time." She looked up at Vaughn. "Unless you want to take over the meeting for me. I'm so glad you're here."

Vaughn looked away from her. "Raven, we need to talk."

Raven studied him more closely. His eyes were red and puffy. He wore the same clothes he'd had on when they'd come home from the cabin, only now they were that much more rumpled from wear.

"Vaughn, what's wrong?" Raven asked.

He shrugged. "I guess I'm confused."

Raven looked straight into his eyes. "About what?"

"Raven! Customer!" Papa yelled.

Raven looked from Vaughn to the trucker who had just sat down at the counter, then back to Vaughn. "Vaughn, hold on, okay?" She took the trucker's order and poured him a cup of coffee. Vaughn stood near the spilled eggs, a frown on his face. An unfamiliar panic was rising in waves through Raven's body. She raced back over to Vaughn.

"Raven," he said slowly, "I—I'm just not sure of my feelings anymore. I don't know. Maybe I really am in SCAM because of how I feel about you, and not the scrublands."

"Vaughn, what are you talking about?"

"Miss!" someone yelled from across the room.

Raven went over and added up another check. She'd thought Vaughn was on her side, that they were in this together. Had it all been a big mistake? She went back to him, suddenly feeling as if he were a stranger.

"I don't know," he said, looking at the mess on the floor. "Maybe my folks are right."

"Oh, your parents." Now Raven understood better. "Is that what this is about? You want to be as perfect a son as your brother, Junior?"

"No. That's *not* it at all," Vaughn objected. "I just think that maybe there are things that are more important than my working for the scrublands. Like my family."

"I see." Raven tried to ignore the bell that told her

115

another order was ready. "But I thought you were the kind of person who stood up for the things you cared about—the things we cared about."

Vaughn shuffled his feet. "Raven, I care about you. I want to be with you. . . ." He still wouldn't meet her gaze. "But . . ."

Raven's stomach sank. Was this how it ended? After a night that she'd thought was just the beginning? Raven had always thought Vaughn was as strong a person emotionally as he was physically. "Don't be a wimp, Vaughn."

"Look, Raven, I sat up all night thinking about this. I didn't come here to fight."

"So what did you come here to do?" Raven felt her voice shaking.

"I don't know. I thought maybe we could talk. Figure this out together."

"Figure what out? Either you do what Mommy and Daddy say, or you don't." Several customers were trying to get Raven's attention, and in the kitchen, Papa was ringing the order bell as if he were playing a drum roll.

"Raven, I thought maybe you'd understand." Vaughn's voice was low, but she could hear the storm clouds gathering behind it. "It's not so simple. The mall is my father's project."

"Gee, thanks for the information," Raven said. "Come on, Vaughn! You're finally doing something

116

good with the mighty Cutter name. Don't chicken out now." And don't fade on me, she added silently.

"My coffee?" yelled the woman at table two.

"I'll be there in a second!" Raven called back to her.

Vaughn's face was red. "I'm not chickening out of anything. They're my family. Don't you understand? I mean, your mother's more important than you chairing the SCAM meeting, right?"

"That's different!" Raven shot back.

"Raven! May I remind you that we're open for business?" Papa called in Spanish.

Raven looked from Vaughn to the plates of hot food Papa had lined up for her, then back to Vaughn. "Your timing couldn't be better."

Vaughn socked a fist into his open palm. "And you couldn't be more sympathetic. Raven, they're threatening to disinherit me."

A bitter laugh rose in Raven's throat. "So you'd wind up just like the rest of us poor slobs?" Out of the corner of her eye, she saw Papa come out of the kitchen in his apron and pick up the orders himself.

Vaughn turned toward the door. "Fine. If that's the way you feel about it . . ."

Raven followed him. "I thought you were a man, Vaughn Cutter!" As she stepped out after him into the open air, her voice grew even louder. "You said you'd never take money for something that was against your principles!"

Vaughn stopped short. "Taking money? You think my family is bribing me?" His volume topped hers, and set the chickens squawking in the wire coop at the side of the café. "It's what I'm entitled to."

"Entitled to be rich? Wow!" Raven said. She shook her head, and her earrings jangled sharply. Maybe she didn't even care if she and Vaughn Cutter broke up.

"No. Entitled to be part of my family. Cutting off my inheritance is like telling me I'm not a Cutter anymore. How would you feel if that happened to you?"

"Well, Vaughn, I don't know how I'd feel about getting cut off from zillions of dollars. I can't say the situation has ever presented itself to me!"

"And so you automatically assume everything my parents do is wrong. Just because they have money." Vaughn's fists were clenched.

"I do know that they have plenty. And that they don't need to be killing the scrublands to get more." Behind them, the scrublands stood as a silent witness to their battle. "I thought you agreed with me."

"Maybe I do. But you seem to think that you and your high and mighty ideals are more important than my family!" Vaughn yelled. "Maybe a mall wouldn't be so horrible after all."

118

Raven couldn't believe that this was the same guy she'd been so in love with the night before last. "Not so horrible. Not if you own it!"

Vaughn bent down and picked up a rock. Raven flinched, raising her hands to her face. Through her fingers, she saw him hurl the rock at the chicken coop with all his strength. It tore through the wire mesh cage and sent the chickens flying in all directions, feathers everywhere, a tremendous squawking filling the air.

"Shut up!" Vaughn yelled, going over to the chicken coop and slamming the wire mesh with his hands. The chickens squawked even louder, and Vaughn pummeled their cage even harder.

Raven felt a stab of shock. "You want to kill something? Is that it? What are you going to do for an encore? Throw a rock at *me*? Or maybe strangle me!" she yelled over the noise.

Vaughn stopped immediately. He looked as if Raven had slapped him. She knew she had gone too far, but fear was pumping through her veins. Then she noticed his bleeding knuckle. The wire had torn right through the skin. Raven froze at the sight of Vaughn with blood dripping down his hand.

But Vaughn didn't even blink. He just turned his back on the whole scene and walked away. He was calm again, but somehow, his calm was just as frightening—no, much more frightening—than his violent fury. When he was angry, at least Raven knew exactly what he was thinking. When he was like this, however, Raven had no idea what he might do next.

CHAPTER 14

Better have that car waiting for me, Manuel.

Lacey was late for school. Again. She managed to brush her hair and put on a pair of dangly crystal earrings at the same time. A quick pencil line to highlight her eyes, a touch of mascara, and . . . There, perfect. Paradiso, here I come. Look out. Lacey got up, grabbed her bag, and hurried out of her room and down the stairs.

She was almost out the door when she noticed that a rose and an envelope with her name on it had been left for her on the side table in the front hall. *Daddy.* She was instantly reminded of the ugly scene with her father that had taken place two nights ago. Her father who might be a murderer.

At least the other night hadn't ended up so badly for Lacey. Calvin was madder than ever, but he was so drunk that he barely had any strength. Besides, he had already taken out most of his anger on the house. When he'd finally gotten to Lacey, he could manage only one little whack of his belt. And it had missed, too. Then he'd just collapsed on the floor, muttering something about T.J.'s famous last words. Lacey felt more shame for him than hatred. He was truly pathetic.

All day yesterday, Cal had been holed up in his bedroom, hungover. He had had the energy, though, to make several angry-sounding phone calls. Lacey didn't need to guess who he was talking to. No doubt he was sending T.J. the D.J. packing—without pay.

She looked at the envelope and started ripping it up. Another payoff. Not again, Daddy. Isn't this ever going to stop? How much did Daddy leave his precious this time? A million dollars? Maybe a blank check. How bad do you think you were last night, Daddy? Lacey shook with bitterness.

She ripped the envelope again and again and spilled the contents out onto the side table, eagerly awaiting the sight of Daddy's million-dollar confetti. Only instead of little bits of green dollars, pieces of multicolored paper with printing on them fell out. Lacey tried to piece the puzzle together to see what precious prize she had just destroyed. She moved the little pieces around on the table. And moved them around some more.

"Stupid!" Lacey shrieked. "Idiot!" Why did it happen this way so often? In her fury at her father, Lacey had just shredded two backstage passes to the Madonna concert!

Completely destroyed. This was catastrophic. Lacey grabbed the rose out of the vase and threw it on the floor, squashing it with her shoe. Then she pulled open the door and slammed it hard behind her.

The car was waiting outside. Lacey ran to it and got in, racing the engine furiously over Manuel's greeting. She peeled off down Winding Hill Road at top speed.

Maybe the Madonna concert wasn't meant to be, Lacey tried to console herself, fighting back tears. But she couldn't understand why every little thing was working against her lately. A few months ago, with the nominations for Peach Blossom Queen, a major portion of Paradiso High was telling Lacey that she was the most beautiful, vibrant, and sought-after girl in school. Since then, it had been nothing but a continuous series of disappointments and letdowns.

Lacey needed an escape from it all. Something to lift her spirits. And she knew just what. She needed a hot date. A night out with someone special. Someone who thought she was special. Someplace far away from Paradiso.

As she roared into the nearly filled student parking lot, Lacey spotted an open space. But as she started to park, another car flew in from the other side. The two cars met face to face, each one taking up half of the space, their tail ends sticking out in either direction.

Vaughn! There's the man I'm looking for, she thought. I'll make him an offer he can't refuse.

Lacey took a deep breath and tried to exhale all the tension. She looked into her rearview mirror, wetting her lips and making sure her makeup hadn't run. You look great, girl, she told herself. Vaughn thinks you're beautiful. How could he resist? Go get him! She beeped her horn and waved. "Hi, sweetie."

Vaughn looked extremely annoyed. "Don't mess with me, Lacey. Not today. I have no patience for you," he snarled.

Lacey laughed. "Vaughn, darling, watch that temper."

"Get your damn car out of my way!" Vaughn yelled. Man, was he cranky!

"I think I was here first, babe. Won't you move for me?" Lacey asked, sugary sweet.

Vaughn wouldn't budge. Lacey knew he was totally worked up. She could practically see steam coming out of his ears.

She got out of her car and walked up to Vaughn's Jaguar. She leaned against the driver's side, elbows on the door, and smiled. "Come on, Vaughn, honey," she purred.

"Lacey, what do I have to do to get you to lay off?"

Lacey studied Vaughn's face. His anger only enhanced his even, chiseled features. His deep-set eyes looked beautiful. "Now, Vaughn, you know I love it when you get so mad. You don't realize how cute you look." Lacey noticed him start to squirm. She had him just where she wanted him.

"Jeez . . . I can't believe you," Vaughn said, shaking his head.

"Relax, will you?" Lacey gave him a playful smile. "It's only a parking space. Where are your manners, anyway? Bet you'd give up that space for Raven. Although I don't think you need a parking space for a burro."

The scowl was back on his face. "Leave her out of this, okay? I don't even want to hear her name right now."

"You don't?" Hope tickled Lacey's heart like a feather. Was Raven the cause of his foul mood? "Is there some reason why you didn't rescue Raven from that little scrubland café this morning?"

"I said drop the subject. Seriously," he warned, releasing an infuriated sigh.

Lacey's heart was pounding. Not because she was scared, but because this was exciting. She noticed a trickle of blood on Vaughn's right hand and a dirty red stain on his white shirt. "What happened, Vaughn, honey? You're bleeding." Lacey reached into the front pocket of her dress and took out her pink silk handkerchief. "Here, let me." She took his hand in hers and started to dab at the wound.

"Lacey," Vaughn spat through his clenched teeth, "I'm fine."

But she held on to his arm. "Hey, relax, will you? Vaughn, you're shaking." Lacey continued to wipe his hand with the silk cloth. She trailed it up the inside of his forearm—the soft, sensitive part—brushing it lightly against his skin.

"Lacey, really. I think we'd better get to school," Vaughn said. But Lacey heard his forcefulness melting away.

She took the handkerchief and wet it with her lips, then returned it to his hand. "There, I think that should do it. Now, what about this parking space?"

Vaughn was finally starting to break down. He shook his head and laughed. "Lacey, you're too much. Really."

"Well, you sure look happier now than you did pulling in here. Let me see that arm again. Just to make sure." Lacey took his arm and ran her fingers over it. "Does it hurt?"

"Lacey . . ."

Lacey held Vaughn's fingertips in her hand. "Vaughn, you may have been steamed a few minutes ago, but I doubt it's anything compared to the way I was feeling. You do have a way of cheering me up, though."

126

"Well, okay, I'll admit it. Same for me," Vaughn said. "Now, what are we going to do about this problem? We can't both park here."

"Okay, Vaughn. It's up to you." Lacey laughed. She threw her car keys up in the air and caught them. "You can have the spot if it's really that big a deal. But I have a better idea," she added as if it were an afterthought.

Vaughn looked skeptical. "Look, Lacey. I've really had a lousy morning," he said, a pained expression starting to show again.

Lacey put a sympathetic arm on his shoulder. "And I've got a wonderful proposition. A great deal to make with you. Really." She gave a slight squeeze.

Vaughn tensed. "Lacey, you may be beautiful, but I don't think of you as the world's greatest diplomat," he said.

Lacey loved hearing the word *beautiful* coming from Vaughn. The rest didn't matter.

She smiled at him. "Listen first. Then decide. Move your car for me, Vaughn Cutter, and I'll take you to the beach in San Diego tonight for a great dinner overlooking the ocean. We'll take my father's jet. I'll even get the pilot to let you fly it."

A mixed look of surprise, excitement, and guilt appeared instantly on Vaughn's face. "I . . . um . . . I . . ."

Lacey squeezed his shoulder. "Just say yes, Vaughn. It'll be a blast."

"Okay, yes. Why not?" he said, grinning.

"I get the feeling you could use a night out away from here as much as I could," Lacey said.

"Definitely," he agreed.

"What's up, anyway?" Lacey wondered what had happened with Raven this morning.

But Vaughn wasn't telling. He just shrugged. Then he said, "Listen, Lacey. About tonight? Nothing serious, right?"

"Now, what does that mean, sweetie?" she toyed.

"No strings attached. Just an innocent little jaunt to the coast. Dinner and then we're home. Right?" he said.

"Innocent? I don't think that I even know the meaning of the word." Lacey laughed, pulling her hands away from him and putting them behind her back. "But don't worry—I'll be good. Promise. You can call me Sister Lacey."

"Well, you don't have to be that good," Vaughn said.

"I'll pick you up at six. We can drive out to the airfield together," Lacey said, getting more and more excited every second.

"I'll be ready," he said.

"Oh, just one thing," Lacey said, remembering her date with Penny. Her ex-date. It wasn't going to be easy to cancel. "Don't tell anybody, okay? Let's just keep this our little secret."

Vaughn nodded. "Sure, Lacey. But—"

"Shhh. For me, Vaughn, okay?" she asked. "Pretty please."

"Okay." He smiled. "For you."

"Yeah. Hey, I gotta run. Do me a favor, babe." She tossed her keys on Vaughn's lap. "I need to talk to Penny about something important, right away. Just park my car and leave the keys under the mat. You can park it over there if you want." She laughed, motioning to another space a few feet away that had been empty the whole time. She bent down and gave Vaughn a little kiss on the cheek. "Thanks. See you tonight, Vaughn." Lacey ran off, leaving Vaughn flustered.

Her head was spinning as she ran up the front steps and headed toward Penny's locker. Maybe this was going to be a great day, after all. All she had to do now was get out of her plans with Penny.

"Penny!" Lacey called down the hall. "Wait up."

Penny was just leaving her locker, walking down the hall to homeroom class. With Hope Hubbard? Boy, Penny must be desperate for someone to gossip to this morning, Lacey thought.

Lacey saw Hope wave good-bye to Penny and rush off as if she wanted to avoid Lacey. Well, that was just fine. Lacey didn't like Hope hanging around her friends, anyway.

"What's up, Lacey?" Penny asked.

"What's up with you, Pen? Hope Hubbard? Since when are you guys pals?"

"I was just telling her about something I saw in the woods behind school this morning. I was taking this new shortcut when—"

"You couldn't wait for me?" Lacey interrupted. "You had to tell Hope first? Such a gossip, Pen."

"Well, it was about *her* cousin. I came across this tree. A pine tree with April and Spike's initials carved into it. A.L. and S.N. forever. With a big heart around it."

"So. What's the big deal?" Lacey asked.

"I thought it might be the murder site, since it's so close to school and all. I figured she'd be interested. You know how she is."

"Hmm. Yeah, I guess." Lacey shrugged. Anyway, she still had to tell Penny about the change in plans for the night. "So Pen, listen. I got some bad news."

"Oh, no. What happened?" Penny said, a look of fright forming on her face.

Lacey faked a pout. "Pen, you're gonna be bummed. But I gotta cancel tonight. We have to reschedule our private party."

"Cancel?" Penny's voice rose. "How come?"

130

"My folks. They said I gotta stay home all weekend and study for finals."

"And you can't take one night off? I've been psyched all week. Besides, when have your parents ever cared so much about how you do in school?" she added, with a bit of suspicion.

"I fought hard for us, Pen, really." Lacey hammed it up as best she could. "But they put their feet down. It was hopeless. I'm not even speaking to them now."

"Great," Penny said. "This stinks. What am I supposed to do tonight?"

"What about Hal?" Lacey took in Penny's angry expression. She thought fast. "How about this? I could give you all my Madonna videos for the weekend and you two can watch them tonight after he wins the match. What do you say, Pen?"

"It won't be the same," Penny said. "Besides, what if he loses today? It'll be horrible, no matter what."

"He'll win, Pen. He always does," Lacey said brightly.

But Penny wasn't smiling. "Hal doesn't even like Madonna."

"Then you can have my other videos too. Any ones you want. And just to show you how sorry I am, I'll send over all kinds of great food. I can have our cook make you guys a feast."

"Yeah?" Penny asked. Maybe it was working.

"And I'll get you some of those fancy chocolates

you love so much for dessert. It'll be real romantic. Just you and Hal and a gourmet feast."

Penny's mood was definitely picking up. Lacey saw a twinkle in her eyes and a smile beginning to form on her lips.

"You'd really do all of that for me?" Penny asked, surprised.

"Of course. You're my best pal, Pen."

Penny's smile was cheek to cheek now. "I didn't mean to get so mad at you, Lacey. I guess I overreacted. I'm sorry."

"I understand, Pen. I'd probably have felt the same if you had to cancel." Lacey put her open palm out to Penny. "Best friends?"

"Definitely," Penny said, giving Lacey a high-five. "Love ya, Lacey."

"Now I'm jealous," Lacey said. "You and Hal are gonna have a romantic feast tonight, and I'm gonna be home alone, reading Shakespeare and studying European history. Thrillsville." Lacey crossed her fingers behind her back. She was proud of her academy award performance and glad she had won Penny back. Now it was Vaughn who needed to be conquered.

CHAPTER 15

This time, Kiki didn't hesitate. First thing Friday morning, she pushed open the door to the art room and walked in confidently.

Mr. Woolery's back was to her as he studied the little painting on the wall over his desk. April's painting.

"It's really beautiful," Kiki said. She summoned up her nerve. "It would be great if everybody in town got to see her paintings," she said boldly.

Mr. Woolery whirled around. "Oh, Kiki!" He looked surprised to see her.

"Hi, Mr. Woolery. I'm sorry I ran out of here the other day," Kiki said, a little sheepishly.

Mr. Woolery let out a long breath. "It's not just you. My class attendance has been way off since . . ." His words trailed off, and he swiveled to give April's painting another glance.

Kiki felt sorry for him. "Mr. Woolery, I guess I owe you an apology."

He shrugged. "It's okay. But what made you change your mind?"

Kiki could feel her face growing red. "A few things." She didn't want to breach Hope's confidence about the investigation she had done on him. Kiki told him the other reasons. "Raven, for one," she said.

"Raven Cruz?"

Kiki nodded. "I'm really ashamed," she said. "But I saw her bracelet on your desk, and she was missing from school and everything. . . . Look, I'm really sorry."

Mr. Woolery gave a sad half laugh and picked up the bracelet. "I get the picture, Kiki. It's all right. There's been a lot of talk. And people are scared. I know you and the other Peach Blossom Queen candidates must be."

Kiki swallowed hard.

"But I picked up this bracelet in the scrublands after Raven dropped it when I ran into her there. I think I frightened her away, too," Mr. Woolery went on gravely. He held the piece of jewelry out to Kiki. "Maybe you could return it to her."

Kiki took the bracelet and slipped it into the pocket of her canvas shoulder bag. "Mr. Woolery? There's another reason I came back in to see you. Like I said when I came in, other people should have the chance to see April's artwork. And buy it," she hinted.

Mr. Woolery nodded. "The exhibit."

Kiki waited for his answer.

Mr. Woolery paced up and down in front of April's painting, studying it. "I feel like I'm looking at the past," he finally said. "April's gone. The scrublands may be gone soon. It's as if the whole town of Paradiso is dying in front of our eyes."

It was a frightening thought. "Mr. Woolery, it might turn out that way. If we keep running away and closing doors and avoiding what's happened. I mean, by shutting yourself away—and shutting April's paintings away—you just make people think the rumors are true."

Same with Spike, Kiki thought. But she didn't say it out loud. Lately everybody except Kiki seemed to think Spike might be guilty.

Mr. Woolery stopped pacing. "And you think that by facing all the talk and going ahead with what I want to do, the truth will come out?"

Kiki nodded.

"Kiki, I wish I could be as optimistic as you are. But the world doesn't work that way." Mr. Woolery sounded old.

Kiki prayed that Mr. Woolery was wrong. "At least think about it. Don't say no right now, okay?"

"I'll consider it," Mr. Woolery said hesitantly. "If they could only find the real killer . . ."

His sentence hung in the air, unfinished.

CHAPTER 16

Hope and Jess followed a barely beaten path through the woods behind school. The midday light filtered through a thick cover of trees, making it seem more like dusk. Dusk in the woods. Hope's hand went to the cut on her cheek. It had partly healed. But the memory of how she'd gotten it was as sharp as the rock that had made the wound. She snuggled closer to Jess, her arm around his waist.

"Hey, you're not scared, are you?" he asked. He stopped walking and wrapped both arms around her.

"A little," Hope confessed, although she felt less frightened in Jess's hug. It was strange, falling in love at a time like this, as if the horror and fear of April's murder had met its match in Jess's warm embrace. Hope was reminded of Newton's law of motion: For every action, there is an equal and opposite reaction.

"We can always go back to school if you want," Jess was saying. "We don't have to go on."

Hope shook her head. "Uh-uh. Blabbermouth Bolton might have given me a clue without even knowing it. That ponderosa pine with the initials sounds like the place where April and Spike used to meet. I mean, unless *you* want to go back," she added.

Jess made a show of pushing the short sleeve of his polo shirt all the way up and flexing his biceps. "Me big, strong swimmer," he joked. "Me not scared of anything."

Hope laughed and rolled her eyes. "You're going to have a pretty hard time swimming away from anyone in the middle of the woods." She took Jess's hand and continued down the path. At the base of a thick blue fir tree, it split in two directions. Hope thought for a moment. "Penny lives over on Caroline Road. That would mean she'd come this way." She followed the right-hand branch of the little path, keeping an eye out for the gray-barked branches and sharp green needles of a ponderosa.

"Hope! Over there!" Jess said after they'd gone a few more yards. He stepped off the path and beat his way through the brambles to a scraggly pine tree. Hope followed him. Her hand on the rough bark, she circled the tree carefully and slowly. She felt a pinch of disappointment. There were no initials.

A bit farther into the woods, however, Hope spotted several more ponderosas, their fallen needles carpeting a sweet-smelling grove dappled by sun and shade. She raced over to one tree, Jess to another. Hope's eyes and hands scoured the gray bark.

Her fingers found a shallow groove in the tree even before she saw it. She pulled her hand back. There was a roughly carved heart. Inside were the initials A.L. and S.N. "Yes!" She gave a cry of triumph.

Jess came running over. He inspected the scar in the tree. "No question about it. This is the place," he said.

Hope took a harder look at the fragrant pine grove, imagining April standing amid the trees, the diffused light softly crowning her red hair. Hope felt so sad. She dropped her head into her chest, blinking back tears. A glint of metal winked at her. Something on the ground was catching a ray of sun. She bent down for a closer look—and she heard herself scream.

A wrench. It was partly buried in the sandy ground. She reached forward.

"Don't touch it!" Jess yelled, moving between Hope and the wrench and grabbing her hand. "Maybe it has his fingerprints on it."

Hope froze. "You mean Spike's?"

Jess sighed. "Who else's, Hope?"

Hope looked down at the wrench, then up at the initials on the tree. "April!" Hope cried, tears streaming down her cheeks.

"Hope . . ." Jess put his arms around her shaking body.

She remembered April's radiant face as she talked about Spike—how sweet and gentle he was, even though most people didn't know it; what a sensitive soul he had under the black leather vest and all his biker's gear. "He's really a teddy bear with an earring," April had said. "Could she have been so wrong about him?" Hope muttered.

Jess lifted her chin up. "I think we ought to go tell the sheriff."

Then Hope recalled the wrench she'd seen in the back of Jess's car, and how she'd almost been convinced that he was the killer. "Jess, what if we're wrong? Like I was about you? You know, all the rumors about Spike may have been what finally made him take off in the first place. And that's my fault."

"For telling the sheriff about him and April?"

Hope nodded.

"Hope, Sheriff Rodriguez would have found out anyway."

"I know. Otherwise I wouldn't have let him get it out of me. Still. What if Spike's innocent and I keep making it look like he's not?"

"And what if he's guilty? He might be April's killer!"

Hope had a terrifying vision of Spike raising the wrench over April's head. She bit back a cry. Then

140

she looked at the heart on the tree again. She thought for a moment. "Jess, maybe you're right. But what difference is it going to make if the sheriff sees this now? No one knows where Spike is anyway. Maybe if we find him—or he comes home on his own—he'll be able to clear up all the stories."

"And if he doesn't? Hope, you've got to face what may be the truth."

Hope nodded. "If they bring him in fighting, we'll give the sheriff that wrench. Let's just wait out the weekend. Maybe something will happen."

Hope traced her cousin's initials. The lines in the bark were slightly gummy with sap. "He's a teddy bear," she heard April's voice say. Then she thought of Spike's father, his hand pressed up against the sheet of plastic at the prison. "Who knows? Maybe they'll find the killer, and it won't be Spike." *But maybe it will be.*

Jess found an old math assignment folded in the back pocket of his jeans and picked up the wrench in it, careful not to let his bare hands touch the tool. As he wrapped it, Hope noticed the bold red *B* at the top of the math paper.

Exhibit B, she couldn't help thinking. *The murder weapon.*

CHAPTER 17

Raven soaked up the afternoon sun as it warmed her back. The scent of peach blossoms hung on the breeze, mixed with a mild smell of chlorine. "Thanks for inviting me over, Kiki. This is great."

"Nothing like lying by the pool like a vegetable. A cure for all ills," Kiki joked. "Maybe you'll feel a little more up for the dinner shift at the café."

"I sure hope so." Raven sat up and took a cold sip of lemonade. "I think Vaughn and I might have scared the morning customers away for good. The jerk." Her blood boiled every time she thought about Vaughn Cutter. She'd avoided him all day at school. But at the same time, she couldn't believe they'd broken up for good. She realized that as she lay by Kiki's pool, she'd been listening for the Jag to come up Winding Hill Road.

"You guys'll make up. I know you will," Kiki said. She slathered some suntan lotion on her fair skin.

"I don't know," Raven said. "It was pretty ugly." She went over to sit by the edge of the pool, letting her long, tanned legs dangle in the water. "Maybe I don't have any business having a boyfriend right now. Too much going on. I probably shouldn't even be here this afternoon."

"Raven, you've got to give yourself a break," Kiki said. "You went home to be with your mother after the lunch meeting, right? And your sister's with her now."

"Yeah. But I'm so afraid of not being there if something happens again. Papa's practically not speaking to me." Raven bit her lip. "I had to lie to him too. I told him Vaughn and I didn't lay a finger on each other. Just fell asleep because we were so tired from everything."

"Oh, right!" Kiki laughed, and shot a crumpled-up napkin at Raven.

Raven laughed too. She could remember how hard her heart had been beating as she lay with Vaughn in front of the fire. Her laughter died in her throat. How could it have gone so sour so fast?

"You'll be back together for the Peach Blossom Festival," Kiki assured her. "I know Vaughn, and I know he's totally fallen for you."

"I'm not even sure that's what I want after this

morning." Raven fingered the turquoise stones on her bracelet. Things had gotten so weird. So weird that Raven had mistaken a glinting object in Mr. Woolery's hand for a weapon, when he was really just retrieving Raven's own lost jewelry. Still, she wasn't a hundred percent sure of Mr. Woolery's innocence in April's murder. She wasn't a hundred percent sure of anything these days. Especially Vaughn.

But Kiki was upbeat. "I *know* you and Vaughn will be going to the Festival Ball together. Maybe he'll be escorting Peggy Sue."

"Or maybe Bobby will be," Raven said. She shielded her eyes from the sun and looked at Kiki.

Kiki shrugged. She came over and joined Raven at the edge of the pool. "Raven, don't tell anyone, but I just don't know about Bobby anymore. I mean, he's the sweetest. He really is. But . . . I just don't think I like him as much as I used to. The thing is, if I break up with him, it'll crush him."

Raven wasn't surprised. She'd had a feeling about this for a while now. "But Kiki, it's not fair to either of you to stay together if you don't think it's right."

"I know. I just keep thinking that maybe Bobby'll start feeling the same way and it won't be so hard. . . . It's so stupid. Here I am with someone I just don't think is right for me, and you and Vaughn are great for each other and you're in this huge fight."

"Maybe we're not so great for each other. He's one

of the Paradiso Cutters, and I'm just a girl from the wrong side of the tracks. Who am I fooling, anyway? Besides, I'm so mad at him, I'm sure if we talked to each other, we'd just get into another fight."

"Boys," Kiki said. She reached for the bag of cookies by her chair. "Want another?"

Raven eyed the bag warily. "If I keep eating those, I'm not going to fit into my dress for the ball. You could probably eat the whole bag and you wouldn't gain an ounce," she said enviously. She went for another glass of lemonade instead.

"One of the advantages of having the figure of a twelve-year-old boy," Kiki said, making a disgusted face. Raven thought Kiki looked great, with long, lean legs and a slender, athletic body, her brown hair streaked with gold by the sun.

"What are you wearing, anyway?" Kiki asked. "Did you sew up something totally awesome?"

"I hope so," Raven said. "I went through a whole stack of magazines from the Fifties to get ideas. It's turquoise taffeta, with a skirt that ends just below the knee—it's got a crinoline under it to make it extra full—and a tight, strapless bodice."

"Sounds hot. Wow, I can't believe you can make something like that yourself. If I had to make my own gown, I wouldn't get to the ball until halfway into the next century."

"And in the seniors' division, Miss Kiki De Santis,

being wheeled in now," Raven joked. "So what's *your* dress like?"

"It's blue chiffon with puffy sleeves and a low neckline." Kiki frowned. "I thought it was really pretty, but then Lacey gave me a hard time because I bought it at a secondhand store."

"Where else are you supposed to get a dress from the Fifties? What's she wearing? Some zillion-dollar brand-new copy of something old and authentic?" Raven couldn't believe Lacey Pinkerton. Anything that wasn't expensive wasn't good enough for her.

"Actually, I think she's wearing the dress her mother wore when she was Peach Blossom Queen," Kiki said. She reached into the bag again.

"Her mom's going to kill her if she doesn't win this time, huh?" Raven said.

Kiki dropped her hand, a cookie halfway to her mouth. "Maybe she's going to kill *us* if Lacey doesn't win. Raven, doesn't the idea of maybe being Queen scare you at all?"

"You mean because the last person named Peggy Sue was killed?" Raven was surprised at how much it *did* frighten her, now that Kiki had brought it up. She wrapped her arms around herself. "I guess with all the other stuff I'm worried about, I've managed not to think too hard about it. I mean, I can't. I need that scholarship money too much."

146

Kiki sighed. "I wish I could throw all my votes to you. I don't even really want to be in the contest."

Raven hoped she hadn't made it sound as if that was what she wanted Kiki to do. Sure, Raven wanted to win, but she'd gotten to really like and respect Kiki lately. "Kiki, listen, let's make a pact that if either one of us wins, we won't let it get in the way of our friendship."

Kiki swallowed and gave a chocolatey smile. "Deal. It's more important than some contest anyway."

"I thought being Queen was like a real dream for you," Raven said.

Kiki frowned. "It is. I mean, it was. Before the murder. But I don't want to wind up dead." She lowered her voice, as if the killer might be right around the corner.

"You know, Kiki, if Spike's guilty like they say he is, the Peach Blossom Queen is safe. He's outta here. Gone. And if he comes back, it's going to be in handcuffs."

Kiki shook her head. "I don't believe Spike did it." She swirled her legs around in the pool. "He may act tough, but I remember one time these guys from San Pedro came into town when I was sitting on the green reading, and you could just tell they were here looking to get into trouble. Anyway, they found me. And they really started scaring me. I mean, there were about five or six of them, and they made this circle around me on the green. Well, all of a sudden, Spike roars up on his Harley. He comes right up on the grass and revs his engine real loud, like he's going to run them over." Kiki's laugh rippled across the pool. "That got rid of them. Spike was really nice to me. He got me a soda and made sure I calmed down, and then he rode me on his bike all the way home. I can't see him as the killer type." She paused. "Killer eyes, maybe." She smiled.

Kiki has a crush on Spike. Raven felt a stab of worry for her new friend. Spike was handsome. And he seemed like Mr. Cool. But he could be a killer. Kiki, however, seemed convinced that Spike was innocent and the real killer was still in Paradiso, just waiting for a new Queen to be chosen.

"Lacey doesn't seem very scared about what might happen to her if she gets to be Queen," Raven mused.

The corners of Kiki's mouth turned down. "She'd probably scare the killer, not the other way around. She's been so horrible lately." Kiki gave a hard kick, and the pool water splashed up. "I know she's never been an angel, but she used to be my best friend. Now she's so wound up—coiled up like a snake, ready to bite."

Raven thought that Kiki was better off without Lacey Pinkerton. But she could see Kiki was hurting. Kiki really was a loyal friend. "It's the murder," Raven

148

said. "Since then, it's like nothing can go right in this town."

Her thoughts went to Vaughn, maybe right next door listening to his stereo or pumping weights in his basement, a bloody rag wrapped around his injured hand. "Nothing."

CHAPTER 18

"What a rush! That's an incredible feeling," Vaughn exclaimed. He was walking back to the main cabin from the cockpit. "Did you see how the plane veered straight up like that when I pulled the throttle out?"

"I could feel it all right." Lacey giggled. "I almost lost my veal Marsala. I think you need a few more lessons before they'll let you go solo."

Vaughn laughed. "I knew this would be a little different than flying the propeller plane my dad and I took up once. This thing cranks!" Vaughn looked around for a place to sit down.

"Right here, Vaughn," Lacey said, motioning to the empty space on the couch. "I won't bite." Lacey was sitting on a plush sofa that faced a small round window. The interior of the jet was done in muted shades of pinks and roses. The salmon pink wall-to-wall carpeting was extra soft. The lighting, controlled by a dimmer switch that was built into a panel next to the couch, was set low. Out the window, Lacey could see the lights that dotted the San Diego harbor fading into the distance. "Look, you can see the moon. It's smiling at us." She patted the cushion.

Vaughn was a little hesitant, but he sat down on the couch next to her and looked out the window too. "Wow. There are a million stars out."

"You know all the names, don't you?" Lacey said, looking out and silently making a wish. *I wish that Vaughn is as into me as I'm into him. This one's coming true. I can feel it.*

"I know a lot of the constellations," Vaughn said, "but I get them confused. I learned them from my father. He learned them looking up from the New Hampshire woods. He claims they're different back East." Vaughn smiled.

Lacey was happy to see him in such a great mood. And to have him here, away from Paradiso, all to herself. "Sorry you came with me?"

Vaughn laughed. "Yeah, it's horrible having dinner on a cliff overlooking the Pacific at sunset. And flying a jet is a drag, too. Thanks, Lacey. Seriously."

"The restaurant was cute, wasn't it? It was fun taking our shoes off and being barefoot like that." Lacey tingled, remembering their feet touching under the cover of the billowy white tablecloth. It had been so

151

romantic, out on the candlelit terrace, looking down at the ocean.

"Everything was great, Lacey. It's really been a blast," Vaughn said.

"What about being with me? Has that been so bad?" she asked coyly, grabbing hold of his arm and taking his hand in hers. She could feel that she had caught him unprepared. He stiffened a little at first. But he didn't object either, so she hung on.

Lacey felt confident that this night was going to keep getting better. They sat quietly, hand in hand, for a while. She lay back on the sofa, resting her head against Vaughn's shoulder, not wanting anything to ever change. Everything felt so wonderful. "What are you thinking, Vaughn?" she asked.

"You really want to know?" he said, a touch of uncertainty in his voice. "I was thinking about my family."

"What about them?" Vaughn's grip had tightened, as he'd said the word *family*.

He spoke softly, but with intensity. "I don't know. I guess I was thinking about how they don't really understand me. They say that everything they do is for my own good. Maybe they mean it, but I think they just can't deal with me being different. They're afraid I'm not a 'true Cutter.' Whatever that is." He frowned. "They're so caught up in the family image.

Dartmouth and all that. I think they're afraid I'm gonna destroy it somehow."

Lacey knew the Cutters. With their old-world, old-money, Ivy League way, they were a different breed of exclusive from her family. Sometimes, they could even be more snobby than the Pinkertons.

"Why would you destroy your family's name? You don't mean to hurt them, Vaughn," she said.

"No, I guess not. I don't know . . ." His voice trailed off.

"Raven," Lacey said. Then she was instantly sorry she had mentioned her name at all. Things were going so well.

There was a long pause. "Yep." He nodded.

His hand tightened even more. It felt a little sweaty.

"They can't stand her," Vaughn admitted. "Never mind." He sighed.

Lacey let it rest. She waited for Vaughn to calm down and get Raven out of his mind. She was hoping he was appreciating how nice their hands were together.

"You know, Vaughn, I'm glad we did this. I was supposed to spend the evening with Penny watching Madonna videos. Well, actually we could have gone to the show, but . . ." She paused and sighed deeply. "Never mind. It's too long a story. Let's just say I've got family problems too. Anyway, it's a lot more fun holding your hand than watching Madonna with Penny." She looked at his face for a reaction.

He smiled. "I'm glad too. Really," he said. "Hey, I think we're flying over the ocean again."

Lacey looked out. "I guess the pilot's just having some fun. He loves to be up in the air. It's so dark down there. Spooky, huh? No one around but the two of us." She sat up and looked into Vaughn's baby blue eyes. "You do look gorgeous, Vaughn."

There was an awkward pause. "So do you, Lacey. I've always thought you were beautiful."

"Then kiss me."

He didn't let go of her hand, but he pulled back.

"What's the matter, babe?" Lacey took her free hand and ran it through his hair. It felt soft. She let her fingers wander, stroking the side of his face. There was no resistance. Lacey gave a seductive giggle.

"Lacey . . ." Vaughn tugged at her hand, but she held on. He could have broken the grasp if he had really wanted to.

"What's the matter, Vaughn? It feels good, doesn't it?" She stroked his face again, drawing sensitive little circles on his cheek.

"But . . ." It was only a matter of time before he gave in to her.

"What's wrong with feeling good once in a while?" Lacey pressed his hand softly. "That's what it's all about, isn't it?" Their eyes studied each other for a moment. An intense moment. She smiled at Vaughn. He couldn't resist. When she reached out for him, he opened up, taking her in his arms, and he joined her in a passionate embrace.

The kiss was blissful. Warm and wet and long. Lacey let her hands run wild through Vaughn's wavy hair, keeping him close. She tickled his neck and face with soft touches, her nails gliding ever so lightly along his skin. His arms were wrapped tightly around her body, exploring the feel of every curve. Lacey was at the edge of control, losing herself in Vaughn.

And then it ended. She felt his body tighten up. Just like that, he stopped. He let go of her.

Lacey's heart sank. "No. Don't stop. Vaughn?" She reached out for him, but he refused her arms.

"Come here, baby. Please. Come to Lacey."

"No." Vaughn turned away. He bowed his head, and covered his face with his hands. "I'm sorry, Lacey. I can't."

"But you feel so good." Lacey pulled Vaughn back into her grasp, wrapping her arms around his waist and pressing her head against his shoulder blades. He felt strong. But he felt tense, too. He was shaking.

"Please, Lacey. I can't." He unfolded her clutching arms. "I know it feels good. To me too. I can't deny that. But it's just not right."

"Raven," Lacey said.

He lowered his head. He couldn't face her. "Uh-huh. I can't get her out of my mind. I'm sorry, Lacey."

Lacey fought, unsuccessfully, to suppress the flood of tears coming on. All her feelings of worthlessness and loneliness were returning. She knew that no matter what she said or did, she wouldn't get Vaughn. Not now.

Lacey flicked a switch on the wooden panel next to the couch, signaling the pilot. "I'd like to go home now," she said, thinking she sounded exactly like her mother when she gave orders to Manuel.

Lacey had nothing to say to Vaughn, who sat on the couch, his head hanging low. He didn't say a word either, except for an occasional weak, "I'm sorry, Lacey."

He should be ashamed, Lacey thought. She felt the sadness he had caused turning to bitterness and anger. Vaughn had let her think that he cared, only to let her down. Her hopes had been shattered. This was supposed to have been a special night. An escape from the mess of a life Paradiso had become. Tonight was for fun and excitement, with no strings attached.

The whole night was ruined. Lacey wished she had never invited him in the first place. Now she would return to Paradiso feeling worse than ever. And the last thing she was going to get when she returned home was sympathy from Mother and Daddy.

CHAPTER 19

I'm going to hate myself for this. Raven walked slowly up Winding Hill Road. Her cheeks were warm with shame at the thought of what she was about to do. She prayed she wouldn't run into anyone she knew on the way.

Especially Vaughn. As she passed the Cutter estate she broke into a jog. Thank goodness for the high stone fence and the long landscaped lawn in front of the house. When she was out of range of Vaughn's property, she slowed down again. She'd gotten by the first obstacle in the course.

The second obstacle was Kiki's house. It was more dangerous, since you could see the road from the house. But from the sounds of it, the whole family was in the backyard by the pool. Raven got by there without being spotted also.

The third and final obstacle was the worst. It wasn't

just a matter of getting by the Pinkertons' without running into Lacey. She had to get all the way inside the Pinkerton mansion. What if she got to the door, and Lacey was the one who answered it? Then she'd have to leave without doing what she'd come to do. A part of her actually hoped that might happen.

She tried to manufacture some handy excuse in case Lacey did open the door. She'd say she was there about the Peach Blossom contest—that she needed to talk to Lacey about it, and about something so important she'd come in person. Hmm, maybe something about security for the three possible Queens until the killer was found. No, that would be using the murder for her own ends. That was what creeps like Calvin Pinkerton stooped to. Cal Pinkerton, damn him.

Raven approached the wrought-iron gate engraved with a curliqued *P*. She'd just have to wing it if Lacey was around. The gate was open, and right inside it, the Pinkertons' chauffeur was washing the limo. Raven recognized him from the day Mr. and Mrs. Pinkerton had come to the café.

"Hello, sir," she said in Spanish. "Is Señorita Lacey home?"

"No, she went out a little while ago," he informed her. Raven felt a breeze of relief. Followed by a queasy, unpleasant realization. She had no excuse anymore. "You want me to tell her you stopped by?"

Raven took a deep breath and shook her head. "No.

Thank you. She's not the person I'm here to see." She made her way to the Pinkertons' front door.

It was opened by a woman in a starched black and white uniform. "May I help you?"

Raven summoned up her courage. "Is Mr. Pinkerton in?"

The woman gave her a look of mild curiosity. "Just a moment." She opened the door wider and let Raven through. "Your name, please?"

"Raven Cruz."

Raven stepped into the marbled foyer, her cowboy boots tapping coldly against the floor. A set of French doors with etched, frosted glass opened on a vast, cavernous room stuffed with showpiece furniture. There was no sense that people really lived here. Raven almost expected a velvet rope to be stretched across the entrance to the room.

"You may wait here," the woman in the uniform said, leaving Raven standing in the foyer.

Raven studied herself in the mirror by the front door. Oval face framed by long, dark hair, large, dark eyes, strong, straight nose, full mouth. She'd half expected to see a different reflection, as if what she was about to do had turned her into someone else. She had a momentary urge to run away. She could still change her mind. But she thought of Mama, weak and feverish in her bed, and she stayed put. The scrubland project was a mess, too. Maybe if those pictures Winston Purdy had taken had turned out to be of an endangered bird, it would have been different. But Raven had just found out for sure that it was only a common robin. Now saving the scrublands seemed even more hopeless than before. And if she was going to lose her battle anyway . . .

The housekeeper returned. "Follow me, please, Miss Cruz," she said formally. She led Raven up the stairs, down a hall of closed doors, and then down another one.

You could get lost in here, Raven thought. And never come out. An image of Calvin Pinkerton wielding a wrench rose up in her mind. The weapon changed to a fireplace poker, and the picture of Mr. Pinkerton was replaced by one of his wife. Raven's body was racked by a violent shudder. She looked behind her, trying to remember the way back out.

"Here you are, Miss Cruz," the housekeeper said. "The door all the way at the end."

At the end. The end, the end . . . Raven willed her feet forward. Every muscle was wound tight. She could feel her heart beating. She knocked on the big oak door.

"Come right in," Calvin Pinkerton's voice called out.

Raven stepped inside the room and found herself in a large study, the walls hung with somber portraits and a heavy, oriental rug on the polished wood floor.

160

In the middle of the room was a huge desk. Behind it, like a king on his throne, sat Calvin Pinkerton, ruddy and jowl cheeked, with a glass of what looked like Scotch in his hand.

"Well, well. Miss Raven Cruz. You've thought about my little offer," he said, his mouth stretching into a seamy smile. "I thought you might."

Raven had to keep the disgust from showing on her face. "I've thought about it."

"And you know what a good education you'll get at Stanford."

"It's not just that." Raven felt her tongue heavy with pride. She made herself speak. "My mother is sick."

Calvin Pinkerton took a swig of his Scotch. "Yes. Yes, I'd heard something about that. And how is Mrs. Cruz?"

"Not good," Raven said. *As if you really care.* "She was sent home from the hospital because my family has no health insurance."

Calvin Pinkerton shook his big head. "Shame," he said. "Crying shame." Raven had a sudden, horrific thought. What if Calvin Pinkerton had arranged to have her mother sent home on purpose? What if he'd just been waiting for Raven to come to him and beg? She might be playing right into his barbarous scheme. But what choice did she have?

"Mr. Pinkerton, my mother is the most important

161

thing in the world to me. Much more important than where I go to college."

"Well, yes. Naturally," Calvin Pinkerton said, standing. "I expect you must be terribly worried about her, and I can sympathize with you, young lady." As he talked, he went over to a portrait of a man who looked to Raven like he must be Granddaddy Pinkerton. He grabbed onto the edge of the frame and swung the painting away from the wall. Behind it was a safe. "No, it just isn't right for a citizen of Paradiso to be denied proper medical care," he said, dialing the combination. He pulled out a wad of green bills and began counting them off.

Raven felt her eyes open wide.

"One thousand, two, three . . . how does five thousand sound?" he asked. He put the rest of the money back in the safe and moved the painting back in place. He waved the five bills in the air. "We'll help poor Mrs. Cruz. Of course we will. Calvin Pinkerton gets great pleasure out of helping the people of Paradiso."

The little people, Raven was sure he was thinking, but she couldn't help staring at the huge sum of money. She gritted her teeth.

"Now, you understand that this is just for starters, my dear." Calvin Pinkerton assumed the tone of a kindly uncle, and Raven felt her stomach turn. "You give me a mall, I'll keep your mother healthy. And you can go to the most expensive college you want. Just as if you were my own daughter."

For a brief moment, Raven actually felt sorry for Lacey Pinkerton.

"Your parents will be so proud," Calvin Pinkerton went on. "Are you the first one in the family to go to college?"

Raven didn't want to admit that she was. She would have liked to bulldoze old Cal and his stereotypes right into the ground. But she was at his mercy. She stretched her hand out to him and watched as he put the bills in her palm. They were crisp and new.

"Oh, the mall is going to be just wonderful, my dear—you'll see," he said.

Did Calvin Pinkerton get pleasure out of making her squirm? Raven closed her hand around the money. Calvin Pinkerton's dirty money. Maybe she was no better than he was.

"I'm glad you paid me this little visit," he said, looking immensely pleased with himself. He tilted his head back and polished off the rest of his Scotch. Raven imagined he'd reward himself with another just as soon as she left.

Her head was spinning as she folded the bills and tucked them into the front pocket of her jeans. Raven had never even seen so much money at once. Five thousand dollars!

Calvin Pinkerton chuckled, and his breath reeked of liquor. "My money will cure anyone."

Raven thought of her mother, her dark hair fanned out on her pillow, her face flushed with fever. "I hope so." She forced herself to thank Mr. Pinkerton.

"My pleasure," he said, with obvious relish. He showed her to the door and closed it behind her. As she walked away from his study she could feel the bills, stuffed in her pocket, pressing against her leg. Her footsteps echoed down the hall as she wondered who else Cal Pinkerton's money had bought and what might happen to somebody whom even Cal Pinkerton's money couldn't buy.

CHAPTER 20

Hope held on to Jess's arm with her right hand. Her left hand was linked with Leanne Hubbard's. She could feel herself drawing courage from their presence on either side of her. Organ music floated out of the white-steepled church and faded on the gentle morning breeze. Hope walked carefully in her cream-colored pumps. She wore them only on special occasions, and she wasn't used to the high heels. She felt grown up in them, and in her tailored linen skirt and silk blouse.

Around them, the congregation of the Church of Christ was arriving for the Sunday service. Hope recognized most of them. There were Mr. Carter, the druggist, and his wife, walking toward the church from the parking lot. Bubba Dole was climbing the church's front steps with his mother. He looked almost tamed in his slacks and tie, his hair neatly combed.

Hope and her mother and Jess made their way up the church's front walk. Hope tightened her grip on Jess's arm as they neared the door. She hadn't been inside Uncle Ward's church in years—not since April had sneaked her inside one afternoon in ninth grade when Saint Ward wasn't there, just so Hope could see what it was like.

April had instructed Hope to sit in the front pew, while she'd taken the pulpit and slipped into her best imitation of her father's somber voice. "Is there anyone among us who did not finish his green vegetables at dinner?" she'd intoned seriously. "Let him stand and confess. Or her." She'd looked right at Hope, and they'd both cracked up.

Hope gave a bittersweet smile as she thought of her cousin. She'd passed the church hundreds of times since then, but the entrance had been barred by the hatred between her family and April's.

But now, finally, Leanne Hubbard had agreed to attend a service and make a gesture of peace toward her brother.

Hope had told her mother Jess's suggestion about going to Uncle Ward's church service. It had taken some convincing, but Leanne had wound up agreeing. Now she looked nervous, her mouth drawn in a tight, tense line. Hope felt the same way. She grabbed even more tightly to Jess's arm.

"Don't worry," he whispered in her ear. "By the way, you look pretty." He kissed her cheek. "Lead me not into temptation," he added jokingly. Hope blushed. Jess knew exactly how to make her feel better.

They went through the open front door of the church and were greeted inside by Mrs. Purdy, Winston's mother. She handed them each a program for today's service. She smiled warmly, if a bit curiously, at seeing them in the Lovewells' church. "I'm so glad to have you with us this morning," she said.

Hope smiled back. Maybe this wouldn't be as difficult as she'd imagined. Maybe the feeling of peace and brotherhood of Sunday services really could be a first step for the Lovewells and the Hubbards. Hope noticed that the programs had a dove printed on the front, an olive branch in its beak. It was a good sign. Peace.

But as Hope was sitting down in one of the rear pews, she felt her nervousness come rushing back. Willa Flicker, from the Paradiso *Record*, was sitting across the aisle, a few rows up. She stared in their direction, and Hope saw her bend over, her right arm moving as she scribbled something in her notepad. Hope prayed that this morning wasn't going to end up as some sensationalized headline in the next issue of the *Record.*

Hope settled into her seat and glared at the back of Willa Flicker's head. She had some nerve coming to church and pretending to be pious and devout, when everyone knew all she wanted was to stir up a dirty story.

Hope wondered what Willa would do with the information about the wrench Hope and Jess had found. She'd have Spike tried and hung before he even had a chance to defend himself, no doubt. The worst part was, maybe Willa would be right about Spike.

No one could believe that Spike had left his little brothers to fend for themselves—but he had. What else would he do that people wouldn't expect? Get April pregnant, for starters. And kill her? Hope wanted desperately to believe in Spike's innocence— for April. But she couldn't stop thinking about the wrench. The weekend was almost over, and Spike still hadn't come home. Nor had another suspect been found. Soon Hope was going to have no choice but to turn the wrench over to the sheriff.

The organ pumped out the first chords of a hymn, and Jess opened his hymnal to share it with Hope. They rose with the rest of the congregation. Hope tried to push the bad thoughts from her mind as she began singing, "Oh, God, our help in ages past . . ."

As the voices lifted to the wooden rafters, all eyes shifted to the back of the church. Uncle Ward was slowly making his way up the center aisle. Hope's heart beat faster at the sight of him. Her voice faded as he grew nearer. She shrank away from him, feeling her mother do the same. But his eyes were forward, fixed on the altar, and Hope and Hope's mother and Jess were way over at the side of the church. Uncle Ward passed by without noticing them. Hope felt a breath of relief. She began singing again. ". . . our shelter from the stormy blast, and our eternal home."

Uncle Ward reached the altar and turned toward the people gathered before him. "The Lord be with you," he said solemnly. Hope noticed that he'd lost weight, and there were circles under his eyes.

"And also with you," the voices around Hope responded.

"Please be seated," Uncle Ward said.

Hope felt Jess close by her as she took her seat again. She slid closer to him as Uncle Ward called on the reader for the day. It was Denise Guthrie, who was in Hope's English class that year. Denise opened the Bible she carried under her arm and began reading the passages noted in the program.

Uncle Ward stood quietly off to the side. Soft light streamed in from the stained-glass windows, throwing rainbow-colored puddles on the floor near Uncle Ward's feet. Hope studied him carefully, noticing the same expression of concentration that April sometimes wore when she was reading a good book or working on a painting or drawing. Hope felt a wave of sadness. She missed April so much. When Denise finished reading, Uncle Ward asked the congregation to say a silent prayer. Hope prayed that Uncle Ward and Aunt Sara would accept her and her mom back into their hearts again and that the feud with April's family would be over.

While Uncle Ward made a few announcements, Hope scanned the church for her aunt. She found her near the front, identifying her by her red hair—almost the color of April's—and her rigid posture. Hope let out a gasp. A few rows behind her aunt sat Renée Henderson—alone and wearing a sweatshirt with a blue hood hanging down her back. Hope grabbed onto Jess's hand. "Jess, look at Renée. Up there, on the left. See? In the blue? The night I got chased—wasn't the person wearing a jacket like that?" Hope tried to whisper, but her voice had a hard, frantic edge to it, and it came out louder than she'd meant it to.

Uncle Ward stopped in midsentence and turned in her direction. Oh, no. He'd heard her whispering. His gaze met Hope's. She saw him take note of Leanne and Jess, too. Hope could almost feel the tension fill the space between them. Uncle Ward swallowed hard and began talking again. But his voice was much tighter than it had been a moment before. "Our father, who art in heaven, hallowed be thy name . . ."

Only as he took his eyes off them did Jess dare to lean over and whisper to Hope, "Lots of people probably have blue sweatshirts. Don't you think?" he added, his voice a bit unsure.

He and Hope traded nervous glances. At the altar, Uncle Ward recited the closing words of the Lord's Prayer. "Forever and ever, amen."

"Amen," Hope echoed automatically with the rest of the congregation. Suddenly, Uncle Ward's gaze was traveling in their direction again.

"Ladies and gentlemen of the congregation, you will notice that the program lists the topic of today's sermon as forgiveness."

Hope felt an unexpected ray of happiness shoot through her. Uncle Ward was talking about forgiveness—and he was looking right at her mother. Hope turned to her mom and saw her eyes open wide, a smile beginning at the corners of her mouth.

"But instead, I'm going to speak with you about wayward souls," Uncle Ward thundered.

Hope felt herself stiffen. Her happiness turned to anger.

"A wayward soul cannot redeem himself—or herself," he added pointedly, "by abandoning our Lord for many long years and then waltzing into a place of worship as if it were a school dance." Uncle Ward's eyes shifted to Hope and Jess, his glance implying that their presence together was some kind of sin. As Hope remembered how Uncle Ward and Aunt Sara never let April dance, she noticed Willa Flicker scribbling furiously. People were shifting around in the pews to look at Hope and Leanne.

Hope sneaked a look at her mother. Her face was red with fury. "We don't have to stand for this," she said, not bothering to keep her voice down. She stood up.

Hope was overcome with embarrassment. Every single eye in the church was now turned toward them. Leanne walked into the aisle, gave her brother a hard stare, and walked toward the doors. She looked back once, to catch Hope's eye. Hope wished she could melt into the floor. Instead, she felt herself rising and following her mother. Her face burned.

"The wayward soul flees in the face of truth," Uncle Ward said into his microphone.

Hope felt her embarrassment spiral into driving anger. How dare Uncle Ward! Her steps were surer as she marched out of the church. Jess was right behind her.

Hope could hear the congregation breaking into heated whispers. Uncle Ward hastily instructed the choir to go into "Amazing Grace." Hope pushed open the church door and stepped into the bright sunshine. "Amazing grace, how sweet the sound . . ."

Hope and her mother and Jess stood dazedly on the church steps.

"I once was lost, but now I'm found . . ." sang the choir.

"Ward Lovewell is the one who's lost," Leanne Hubbard said, her voice low with anger.

Hope blinked against a rush of tears. Her thoughts were dark and confused. They flitted from one sad and frightening place to another. Her mother. Uncle Ward. April. Spike. Wherever he was. To Hope, it felt as if the entire town of Paradiso were lost.

CHAPTER 21

Stop crying. You gotta stop it, Lacey kept telling herself. She sat at her dressing table, a makeup brush in her hand. As the tears streamed down the side of her face, they took the heavy cover of blush with them. Lacey was struggling to cover up her black eye.

It was the most recent present from Daddy. She had received it late Friday night, upon returning from the miserable adventure in San Diego. As if the night with Vaughn hadn't ended badly enough. But there was Calvin, drunk as usual, waiting for her at three o'clock in the morning. This was the worst yet. It was the first time he had ever hit her in the face. Where would it end?

Lacey stared at her reflection in the mirror. She wished the black eye would disappear. Instead she had to cover it up, like she had to do with all her problems.

Lacey knew that deep down her father loved her.

She thought about the special trips that the two of them took on the jet. San Francisco for dinner. Hawaii for the weekend. Paris! She was the most treasured thing in his life. So why did he do this to her? He needed help. Serious help.

With every new application of makeup, a fresh flood of salty tears would uncover the big black-and-blue patch. It was useless. It doesn't matter anyway, she thought. Everybody knows already. Damn that Willa Flicker.

Lacey glanced at the crumpled-up copy of the *Record* on her dressing table. There it was on page one, a giant photo of Lacey, an astonished look on her face, with a poorly camouflaged black eye. Lacey had tried to go shopping in Sacramento to avoid having to face anyone in Paradiso. But Willa Flicker had somehow caught Lacey in Sacramento. She always seemed to be around to catch you at your worst. She had some kind of sixth sense.

The accompanying article was equally devastating. Lacey reread the headlines —BLACK AND BLUE: MURDER FOR A MALL. THE PINKERTON CONNECTION it said, in slightly smaller letters. And the caption beneath the photo asked, "Could the person who did this be capable of murder?" Lacey was sure everyone in Paradiso had snatched up the paper immediately to find who had done it. Well, they aren't going to find out, she promised herself.

175

But Lacey was afraid that Willa Flicker was starting to figure things out about the Pinkertons. Her scathing piece focused mostly on Calvin and how much power he had. And she'd implied that he was enough of a monster to give his own daughter a black eye. The article went on to suggest that Calvin was involved in organized crime. According to Willa, Calvin wouldn't stop at anything to gain money and power. She had in essence accused Calvin of April Lovewell's murder.

Still, Lacey knew Willa was only taking a vicious stab at her family to sell more papers. And to bolster her sleazy little career, if you could call it that. She had no proof. The only real facts in the story were that Lacey's father had gotten T.J. the D.J. fired, and that Lacey had somehow gotten a black eye.

Lacey dreaded having to live the day that awaited her. Paradiso would be rocking. She was sure that she'd be the center of attention. That was nothing unusual. But today, she would have to answer to all the kids hounding her to fess up. What could she tell them? How was she going to face them all? With sunglasses, for starters.

Lacey made one more futile attempt to cover up the shiner. Her wastebasket was already half filled with the tissues she had used to wipe up each failed effort.

She reached for the newspaper. Furiously, she took

her makeup brush and blotted out her eye in the photo. Then she ripped up the paper and stuffed it in the wastebasket.

I hate you, Willa Flicker! I hate this whole damn town!

For the first time since she got her license, Lacey drove slowly to school. The few people she noticed as she pulled into the parking lot seemed to avoid facing her directly. She was sure she heard someone shouting, "Here she comes!" as she got out of the car.

They were all waiting for her on the front lawn. Everyone. Lacey could feel the tension build as she got nearer.

"Here comes Killer Lacey."

"She did it."

"Check it out, the killer's daughter."

"It's beauty and the beast, all in one!"

"Hey, Champ, what's behind those shades?"

Actually, wearing the dark sunglasses, Darla style, helped to filter out some of the commotion, and allowed Lacey to feel a little distanced from the scene. Lacey had a sudden understanding of what her mother was all about.

Then, as Lacey made her way to the school's main entrance, she saw the worst part. Willa Flicker, in the flesh. All 250 pounds. Lacey trembled. The photographer from the Sacramento nightmare was at Willa's side. Like warriors prepared to do battle, they were waiting eagerly. As Lacey approached, Willa positioned herself right in front of Lacey, blocking her path. Lacey moved to her left to try to avoid her, but Willa moved with every step. The camera started to click away.

"Care to make a comment, Ms. Pinkerton? For the citizens of Paradiso?" Willa's voice had such fake concern.

"Leave her alone! Haven't you done enough damage already?" Renée stepped between Lacey and Willa, making Willa jump back.

Thank God Renée's so tall, Lacey thought. Penny was there too. Lacey felt protected.

"You're a horrible woman!" Penny shouted. She turned to Lacey. "Don't worry, Lacey."

"Thanks, guys. I knew I could count on you," Lacey said.

But Willa wouldn't budge. Lacey looked around. An entire school full of kids were hanging around, gawking. All the chatter was producing a whirring buzz that made Lacey feel like she was about to be attacked by a swarm of killer bees. And Willa was queen bee.

Out of the corner of her eye Lacey noticed Raven sitting alone under a tree. She had a book in her hand and was pretending not to pay any attention to all the commotion on the lawn. Farther away, Lacey saw Vaughn, leaning against one of the stone pillars on the front steps, no doubt feeling sorry for himself, deep in misery over losing Raven. The kids on the lawn were yelling at Lacey—"Who did it?" "Who's the killer?" "Come on, tell."

Lacey whipped her sunglasses off to reveal the black eye. "Okay. I'll talk. You want to know who hit me, right?"

"If you would, Lacey. Who did it to you?" Willa asked, giving the photographer a nudge and motioning to him so that he would move in for a close-up. "Start shooting," she muttered to him. "Don't miss a thing."

"Vaughn," she said softly. She noticed Penny and Renée's stunned reactions. More loudly she shouted, "Vaughn! Vaughn Cutter!" Lacey heard the hum grow louder. The bees of Paradiso had plenty to buzz about now.

Willa gasped. "Of course! That explains it. Oh, my God. That's the missing link."

"What are you talking about?" Penny snapped.

"The check. The money Lacey Pinkerton paid Vaughn Cutter. That explains April's murder."

Lacey was stunned. She froze for a minute. *You idiot. That check had nothing to do with April Lovewell. But Daddy will go crazy if he finds out I gave Vaughn that money to have my car fixed. Plus, they'll attack Daddy in the papers again. They'll make him look dangerous. That's exactly what they want.*

179

"How do you know about that check?" Lacey finally asked. "Who told you?"

"I have my sources. I know you paid Vaughn five hundred dollars," Willa stated. "A pretty modest amount for a contract murder, I might add."

A cry came from the crowd. "Oooh. Vaughn and Lacey are partners in crime." It was Eddie Hagenspitzel. "I'll bet those big feet of hers fit the prints, too. Yep. Vaughn killed her and the two of them dragged her to Hope Hubbard's locker. Clever." So Eddie had found a way to get back at Lacey for being so cold to him the other day. His remarks were followed by a slew of shouts and condemning remarks.

"She did it!"

"Vaughn and Lacey are the killers!"

"They're dangerous!"

Lacey's head spun. "You can all shut up!" she shouted. "That means you, Hagenspitzel. And you too, Flicker. You don't know what you're talking about. I didn't do a thing."

Willa laid into Lacey. "Maybe you didn't, Lacey. But that doesn't mean your father is innocent. Stop playing games. You can't cover up for him forever, you know. I know that money came from Calvin Pinkerton. And I suspect Vaughn was going to confess, and you tried to stop him. To save your precious family."

"No!" Lacey covered her head in her hands.

"Don't you see? You were used, Lacey. As a front.

180

Used, just like he uses everyone and everything in this town." Willa spoke with conviction.

"Shut up!" Lacey yelled.

But Willa was on a roll. "I always knew about your father, Lacey. It didn't surprise me a bit when he fired T.J. the D.J. But having April Lovewell killed to drive home a point in an advertisement? Just for a mall? Tsk, tsk, tsk," Willa clucked.

Enough. Lacey pulled her hand back and took a swipe at Willa. Willa shrieked. Lacey pushed with all her might, sending her to the ground, her pad and pencil flying. The whole time, the photographer's automatic winder whirred away.

Lacey looked down at Willa. She felt her heart pounding. But it gave her satisfaction to know that Willa's was beating even louder.

"Like father, like daughter," Willa said, looking up at Lacey. "I see Calvin has taught you well."

"I'll get you for this, Flicker." Lacey looked at the crowd, which had formed a tight circle around her and Willa. "Well, I don't know about you guys, but I don't want to be late for school." Lacey turned and ran up the steps.

"Go to jail!" Eddie Hagenspitzel shouted as kids started following Lacey into school. "Go directly to jail. Do not pass go. Do not pay Vaughn Cutter five hundred dollars."

181

CHAPTER 22

Sheriff Rodriguez rapped on the already-open door to Mr. Raleigh's European history class and came in accompanied by two policemen.

"The troops have landed!" Eddie Hagenspitzel called out.

Hope began to laugh. Then she noticed the shorter of the two policemen had his hand on the gun in his holster. She was instantly quiet.

"Vaughn Cutter?" the sheriff said, searching the room with his eyes until he found Vaughn. Hope shifted in her seat to look at him. Everyone else in class automatically did the same.

"Yes?" Vaughn answered warily.

"Come with us, please," the sheriff said.

"Excuse me?" Vaughn didn't move. "For what?"

Hope had heard by now about the scene in front of school that morning. She'd also heard that Vaughn had denied touching Lacey.

At first, Hope was doubtful. She'd seen Vaughn's hot temper in action before. Everyone had. But the more she thought about it, the more she believed Vaughn. It just wasn't Vaughn's style to hit girls. Walls, furniture, Bubba Dole, sure.

Hope waited for the sheriff to accuse Vaughn of blackening Lacey's eye. She wondered if Mr. Pinkerton had sent these guys. But the sheriff had much more shocking news. "Vaughn Cutter, you're under arrest. For the murder of April Lovewell."

A blade of shock sliced through Hope's consciousness. Gasps and whispers spread through the classroom.

"I don't believe it!"

"I knew it!"

"It's a setup!"

Vaughn jumped to his feet. "It's a lie!" he yelled.

The sheriff made a motion and the two officers came toward Vaughn, grabbing his arms. Vaughn struggled to free himself. "What proof do you have? You can't do this!" His eyes flashed with fury. He fought like a trapped animal.

"I have a copy of a certain check you were issued by one Lacey Pinkerton," the sheriff said. "It would be better if you came without fighting," he added. The shorter of the policemen managed to clasp a pair of handcuffs around Vaughn's wrists.

"That check was—"

"You'll have plenty of time to explain yourself at the station," the sheriff interrupted Vaughn. "But I'd advise you to wait until you have proper legal council before speaking, Mr. Cutter," he said formally.

How many times had the sheriff rooted at one of Vaughn's wrestling matches? Or joked with Lars Cutter at a town meeting? And now he was bringing Vaughn in for murder!

"You don't understand!" Vaughn was saying as the policemen led him out of the classroom.

Hope heard one of the officers reading Vaughn his rights as they walked down the hall. This was unbelievable. Hope shuddered. What if they had the wrong man, and she and Jess were hiding the evidence that could prove it? Hope couldn't wait any longer. It was time to come clean with Sheriff Rodriguez, even if it meant further implicating Spike. There was no other choice. Hope couldn't protect him any longer. Not at the expense of someone who might be innocent.

She felt herself standing up. "Excuse me, please," she said in a weak voice. "I have to go." Hope ran out of the room, not even answering Mr. Raleigh's demand for an explanation.

She had to catch up with the sheriff and tell him about the wrench. Now. And she had to admit that he might have been right about Spike Navarrone.

CHAPTER 23

Raven could hear all the chatter coming from inside the classroom where she'd scheduled the SCAM meeting. "Yo, man, if Willa Gorilla had given the scrublands as much press as Lacey's black eye, maybe we could drum up enough support to actually do something," she heard someone say.

"Do you think Vaughn really did it?" Raven recognized Emily Gilman's voice. "I heard he and April had something going behind Spike's back."

"Yeah? If you believe rumors, April had something going with almost everyone."

"I don't believe it," Kiki said.

"Yeah, that's what people were saying about me, last week. All they're doing is recycling the rumor with someone else's name," Jess Gardner agreed.

"Well, then why did they arrest him?" Janice Campbell asked nasally. "He must be guilty."

"Partners with Spike," someone else added.

Raven wanted to plug up her ears and run in the opposite direction. All she'd heard since first thing this morning was Vaughn, Vaughn, Vaughn. Vaughn was a psycho killer, or at least vicious enough to punch a girl in the eye. Vaughn was innocent, the victim of Lacey's rage. Vaughn was being paid off by Calvin Pinkerton to take the heat for Calvin's crime. Or for his wife's.

Raven didn't know what to believe. Could Vaughn really have hit Lacey? He'd gotten mad enough at her once before to kick a hole right through the wall of his family's cabin. And the rock he'd hurled through the chicken coop outside the café could have killed one of the chickens. Yeah, he might have done it.

But murder? That was just too much for Raven. Vaughn, a murderer? The boy in whose arms she'd felt such happiness only a few nights ago? The boy she missed so much it hurt—despite the anger she still felt toward him? How could he be a killer?

Raven leaned against the wall outside the classroom. What if something had happened by accident? What if it was true about April and him? What if he was the one who had gotten her pregnant . . . and he was afraid to tell his parents? Raven knew all too well how much Vaughn thought he had to live up to for his mother and father.

Why couldn't time have stopped at the cabin,

186

frozen in a perfect night? Since then, there had been only pain. Mama's illness, the trouble Raven was in at home, the fight with Vaughn, the money from Calvin Pinkerton—and now all the rumors Raven wanted desperately not to believe.

Inside the classroom, the talking continued.

"Where is Raven, anyway?" came Winston Purdy's voice.

"She'll be here," Kiki said loyally.

"It's not like her to be late," Winston said.

Raven knew she had to face the other members of SCAM. She took a deep breath and went into the classroom. She took her place at the front of the room.

"How's your mom?" Winston asked.

"She's—resting," Raven said gravely. Then, "Listen, guys, I've got to talk to you." Her words came out in a jumbled rush. There. She'd said it. Now she couldn't chicken out. All eyes were on her. "I—I can't be part of SCAM anymore."

There was a startled silence. Finally, Winston's voice rang through the room again. "Part of SCAM? You *are* SCAM."

Raven swallowed hard. She studied the linoleum tiled floor. "I'm under a lot of family pressure," she said softly. "On top of the murder, the end of school coming up, the Peach Blossom contest . . ." She didn't add Vaughn to the list, but she couldn't stop thinking about him, either. "There's a lot going on." She pictured the stack of crisp thousand-dollar bills she'd hidden so carefully in a box of baby toys that all her brothers and sisters had grown too old for. Her face grew hot with shame.

"Everyone's got a lot going on," Kiki spoke up from near the front of the room. "But the scrublands are the most important. You were the one who showed us all that." Raven couldn't meet Kiki's eye. Kiki was absolutely right. Raven was sacrificing everything she believed in. But then she thought of Mama and launched into the speech she'd written the night before and memorized.

"Yes, it would be great to have nature all around us."

The room filled with cheers and hoots of agreement. "Right on!" someone yelled. Raven was filled with guilt.

"But I've learned a lot recently about power and money."

"Boo! Hiss!"

Raven felt like the biggest traitor since Benedict Arnold. "It's not the people against the enemy," she said. "It's the little kids against millions of dollars and big machines. Maybe if the bird Winston had photographed had turned out to be endangered, we'd have had a chance . . ." Raven heard her words coming out flat and fake to her own ears, but she pushed on.

188

"Maybe in the end we'll feel just fine with a mall . . ."

She made the mistake of looking up at the people in the room. Winston Purdy's face was twisted in shock and disappointment—disappointment in Raven. Some of the kids looked angry or downright disgusted. But what hurt most was Kiki's reaction.

"What about the ozone layer and the animals?" she said.

"And the trees?" Winston added.

"The birds?"

"Everything we've been fighting for?"

Raven had no answers. No good answers. "I'm sorry. I'm really sorry." She made a move for the door.

"That's all? You're just quitting?" Winston yelled.

"Hey, Raven, what gives?" Jess Gardner asked.

Raven could feel her eyes stinging with humiliation and frustration. "I can't help it . . ." she blurted.

She fled from the room without looking back.

CHAPTER 24

Lacey leaned against the wall of metal gym lockers. She was red in the face and breathing hard, fighting to catch her breath.

"It was only two laps around the gym, Lacey," Penny teased.

"Give me a break, Pen." Lacey wiped the sweat from her brow. "Not everyone is a jock like you."

Lacey got up and took her dress and tights out of her locker. Without saying a word, she headed for one of the private stalls, hoping Penny wouldn't ask any questions. Lacey couldn't wait to get dressed and go home. This had been one of the most humiliating days ever. From the moment she set foot on the front lawn of school, she had received nothing but dirty looks and accusations from practically the entire student body. Murderer. Accomplice. Daughter of a murderer. Ex-girlfriend of a murderer. No matter whom they accused, Lacey was involved.

Lacey thought about her encounter with Willa Flicker earlier that morning. It would probably be on the front page of the *Record*. What would the article say this time? How much worse could it get? And what would Daddy do in response to the embarrassment the article would cause the family?

Mother and Daddy. Lacey shuddered. Pulling her tights up over her legs, she felt a dull pain. It was nothing compared to the ache she'd feel if people saw the bruises. The reaction to her black eye gave Lacey an indication of how people might respond to seeing her marred legs. At least everyone still thought Vaughn was the culprit.

But Daddy's the real horror, Lacey thought. He was the one who was responsible for Lacey having to sneak into the bathroom to slip on a pair of tights.

"Hey, get out of here!" a voice screamed from the showers.

"Girls only, jerk!" another angry girl shrieked.

As Lacey returned to her gym locker, she saw Eddie Hagenspitzel being chased out of the locker room. A group of half-dressed girls were flinging their wet towels at him.

Penny was laughing. "What a perv. Boys never grow up."

"I'm glad I missed him," Lacey said. She stuffed

her sweats back in her locker. "Hey. Where's my shoe? One of my shoes is missing."

"Hagenspitzel!" Penny gasped. "He stole it right out from under my nose! I didn't even see him."

Lacey's face returned to the deep red it had been just a few minutes ago. She remembered Eddie's comment earlier about her feet being the same size as the murderer's.

"I'll kill him," Lacey fumed. She bolted out of the locker room, the lone shoe in her hand.

"Where's Hagenspitzel?" Lacey asked Hal Bemis, who was walking out of the boys' locker room. "Which way did that fat worm go?"

Hal pointed in the direction of the main entrance to the school. "Better hurry, Lacey. He was moving fast. Like he was on a mission."

Lacey ran down the hall. When she found Eddie, he was standing by the front door, holding the shoe up high over his head. A crowd had gathered around him. And Willa Flicker was among them with her cameraman loyally by her side.

Eddie was hamming it up for every possible "ooh" and "ah." "Step right up, folks, and get a firsthand look at THE shoe. The largest shoe ever belonging to a murderer. Female murderer, that is. Yessirree, this is it, everyone. No doubt about it. Step right up and see for yourselves."

Lacey didn't know what to do. She held the other

shoe behind her back, shielding it from view. Lacey caught Eddie's eye. The look on his face told her he was not about to stop.

He pointed to Lacey. "There she is, folks. The pretty little lady with the big feet. Missing something, Lacey? I think I found it. Or is it Noah's lost ark?"

Lacey was speechless. She was too embarrassed to claim the shoe. But her cover was blown already. Standing there barefoot, and obviously hiding something behind her back, she was a dead giveaway.

She was right back where she had been earlier the same day. Everybody's object of ridicule. Now she had to bear the smirks and nasty comments of the onlookers. She did all that she could to block out the chorus of "She's the one," "Prettiest darn murderer I've ever seen," and "Big foot strikes again!"

There was an extra burst of excitement as somebody spotted Vaughn coming through the front door to the school with Hope. Vaughn looked livid.

"Here comes Lacey's cohort, the jailbird!" someone shouted.

"Who sprung him loose so quickly?" another voice yelled.

"Did Calvin Pinkerton pay your bail, Vaughn?" Bubba Dole quipped.

Vaughn barreled through the crowd, pushing aside anything that got in his way. "Out of my way, Bubba. I'll deal with you later." He came right up to Lacey and grabbed her arm, yanking her around to face him. "I hope you're satisfied now. You almost put me in jail, you liar."

"What's the matter, Vaughn?" Eddie asked. "Did Lacey's check bounce?"

The crowd roared with laughter.

Vaughn gave Eddie a threatening look. "You want to eat that shoe?"

Eddie turned bright red. "I didn't mean it."

Lacey tried to yank herself free from Vaughn's grip. But he wouldn't let her loose. "Leave me alone, Vaughn. You're hurting me."

Obeying Willa Flicker's orders, the photographer focused in close on Vaughn and Lacey.

"Vaughn, stop." Lacey tried to scratch at Vaughn with her free hand, but he grabbed it and twisted it around her back. "Let me go," she pleaded.

"Not until you admit the truth. Come on, Lacey. Tell them about the check. Tell them that the money wasn't from your father. It was to keep him away!"

Willa was there, front and center, enjoying every little juicy detail to the fullest.

Lacey was in tears. "Vaughn, stop!" With all her strength she pulled herself away, falling backward with such force that she caromed off the photographer and fell to the ground.

But Vaughn wouldn't let up. He was furious. He looked down at Lacey. "Tell them, Lacey! Tell the truth. Tell them how that money was used to pay Jess for fixing your car. You paid me so that your father would never know what you'd done. And you were too embarrassed, after you broke up with Jess, to ask him yourself. You knew he was too mad at you to do it unless I convinced him. Go ahead. Tell them, Lacey."

Lacey lay on the ground crying as Vaughn stormed off. *Why doesn't everyone leave me alone? I can't stand it anymore.* The noise level had reached thunderous proportions. The camera continued to click away.

"That's enough!" Principal Appleby was outraged. "Ms. Flicker, out. You are trespassing. Leave these premises at once. And take the photographer with you. If I see one picture of this school in the paper, you will force me to consult a lawyer. You will not turn my school into a gossip headquarters. Out!"

"But Mr. Appleby. The evidence!" Eddie Hagenspitzel held up Lacey's shoe.

"I'll take that." Mr. Appleby grabbed Lacey's shoe. "If you'll excuse me." He pushed through the crowd and made his way to Lacey. "Here you are, Lacey."

The crowd had quieted to a low hum. Lots of "shhh's" and "quiet's" as Mr. Appleby commanded attention.

"I am shocked. I used to think of my school as a model of what a stimulating academic and social environment should be. What's gotten into you all? I

195

thought you were groovy high school students. Not babies. You guys are bumming me out. From now on, in my school, you will behave like the young adults that you are. Or else."

"Or else what?" someone blurted.

Mr. Appleby was flustered. "I mean it, dudes. Stop the games." He turned and walked away, leaving an anxious crowd unsure of what to do next.

"The Dweeb is right!" Penny shouted. "We're all blaming everybody else, because we've been avoiding the real murderer."

"There she is!" cried Eddie, pointing to Lacey. "Just measure the foot."

"Don't be a fool, Hagenspitzel," Penny said. "Lacey's not the killer."

"What makes you so sure?" asked Janice Campbell, poking her head up from behind Eddie.

"Because I know who did it," Penny said, hushing the crowd to a whisper.

"So tell us, then," Janice said quietly. "Who killed April, Penny?"

Penny looked nervous. Lacey picked herself up off the floor. All eyes were on Penny. She wrinkled her face in a tight frown. "Well, the murderer is . . ." Was she searching for a name? "Spike Navarrone," Penny finally said. "Isn't it obvious? You all remember him, don't you? April's boyfriend? The father of her baby? The one who's missing. The one who the police still have an APB out on."

"I don't believe you," brutish Bubba Dole squawked, stepping up to Penny. "I liked Spike," he snorted.

"Yeah," Eddie backed him up. "How do we know you're not just covering up for Lacey? Like you always do."

Come on, Penny, keep fighting for me, Lacey prayed.

"You're so stupid, Hagenspitzel," Penny sneered, waving a fist at him. "First of all, Lacey's got an alibi. She was with me the night April was murdered. I slept over at her house that night. We were together all night. So you can forget about blaming Lacey." Penny went over to Lacey and put a supportive arm around her. "Come on, Lacey, we don't need this. Let's split."

Lacey followed Penny out the door, quivering at the sounds of the snickers and hisses.

"We still love you, Lacey."

"I'll visit you in Folsom. Promise."

"Don't worry, Lacey. With any luck at all, you'll be out by your fortieth birthday."

"Stay away from your father, Lacey. He's the real killer."

CHAPTER 25

Kiki clutched a bouquet of purple and yellow tulips close to her heart. The cemetery was quiet and empty, a world apart from the way it had been when a shocked crowd had gathered for April's funeral. It smelled of freshly cut grass, and as Kiki made her way to April's grave, she found herself thinking that the cemetery was like a carefully manicured lawn that bloomed with gravestones instead of flowers.

Kiki wondered how many of her classmates had made this visit. April hadn't even been dead for two weeks, but it sometimes seemed as if she were already consigned to the past. Sure, the murder was still the major topic of conversation, but it seemed like one part fear and one part gossip. Where was the part about April Lovewell the person? Where was the part about someone who was gone? Kiki and April hadn't been all that close, but Kiki had liked April Lovewell

—and she felt sad that she'd never be able to get to know her better. With all the talk about the murder, Kiki felt it was only right to pay a visit.

She trod softly across the grave sites to where April was buried. It should be right about there, blocked from view by the thick trunk of a peach tree, bursting with snowy blossoms. Kiki buried her nose in the tulips she had bought for April and breathed in their perfume for comfort.

Suddenly, she heard a male voice rising in despair from the direction of April's grave. "I'm sorry!" he cried out. "April, I'm sorry!"

Kiki's heart skipped a terrified beat. She had company in the cemetery. Someone who was sorry for something he'd done to April! The killer! Her pulse raced with fear.

And then she saw him as he shifted position and was no longer fully hidden by the peach tree. Even from the back, his leather vest and dark thick head of hair were instantly recognizable. It was Spike. He *was* the murderer.

Kiki let out a panicked gasp. Spike turned toward the sound. Kiki's legs seemed to move on their own. Her feet pounded against the grass. Horror rose up in her throat as she ran.

"Kiki!" She heard Spike yell. She ran as hard as she could. The tulips fell from her hands. "Stop! Kiki!" His voice was getting closer. He was coming after her!

Kiki wove through the tombstones. She pumped her legs, but they were weak with fear. *Go!* she told herself. *Faster!*

But her own scream split the air as she felt herself grabbed by the arm. "Kiki," Spike said.

Kiki was gasping for breath. His face only inches from hers, Spike was breathing hard too. "Please," he said, "please, Kiki, don't turn me in. I didn't kill April." Kiki saw that his eyes were moist.

"But I heard you. I heard you apologizing to her, Spike. And they know about the wrench that you used." *Don't kill me too,* she prayed silently. *Help me, someone!*

"You've got it wrong, Kiki," Spike said. "You've got to believe me. I *am* sorry for April. Yeah. Sorry I loved her so much that I got her pregnant. Sorry I couldn't protect her from the killer. Sorry I hurt so bad I don't know what to do . . ." Spike's voice cracked. Beads of sweat stood out on his face, and he seemed as scared as Kiki. She looked into his large dark eyes and found herself believing every word he was saying.

Then she took a step back, breaking free of his hold. April had looked into those dark intense eyes too. April had believed in Spike. And now . . . Kiki's gaze shifted to the spot where April was buried, then back to Spike. "If you're innocent, why did you run away?"

Spike gave an empty laugh. "I wish I could have

run away. All the rumors, all the feelings I couldn't handle—can't handle now . . . but I never got past the county line."

Kiki studied him, trying to gauge whether he was telling the truth.

"My little brothers—I couldn't split on them." Spike made no attempt to grab hold of Kiki again. "I couldn't split on April, either." His voice got teary. He paused a moment and swallowed back his pain. "I've been hiding out in the woods behind our trailer," he said. "There's an abandoned car on our property. At night, I sneak in there and sleep. My brothers swore not to tell. As little as they are, they know this isn't a game."

Kiki heard the tenderness in Spike's words. How could a guy like this be a murderer? She faced him silently. He held her gaze.

Suddenly, the moment was shattered by the wail of sirens. The police! Spike began to run. Kiki called after him, "Don't, Spike! You'll just make it worse! Stay while there's still a chance!" Spike slowed down and looked over his shoulder, but he didn't stop.

Kiki began to follow him. "If you run, you're admitting you're guilty!" she yelled over the sirens. "Spike!"

He stopped and looked at her, then turned toward the sirens. They grew louder and louder. Over by the cemetery gate, two cars with flashing lights squealed to a halt.

201

"If you're innocent, stay and defend yourself," Kiki pleaded as she caught up with him. She held out her hand.

Spike reached toward her. She felt an electric tingle as their fingers met. By the gate, the sheriff and two police officers were getting out of the cars.

Spike pulled his hand away. Suddenly, he was running again.

"Spike!" Kiki called. She put her hand to her lips. He kept going, weaving wildly between the tombstones, as if he were running for his life. Then he was gone.

Official Rules:

1. Mail your entry to "Who Killed Peggy Sue" Contest, Puffin Books Marketing Department, 375 Hudson Street, New York, NY 10014. One entry per person. 2. Entries must be received no later than November 18th, 1991. Puffin Books is not responsible for misdirected or lost mail. 3. The winner will be chosen in a random drawing. The winner will be notified by mail. 4. This contest is open to all U.S. and Canadian residents over the age of 12 as of January 1, 1991. Void where prohibited. Employees of Penguin USA (and their families), their respective affiliates, retailers, distributors, and advertising, promotion, and production agencies are not eligible. 5. Taxes, if any, are the responsibility of the prize-winner. Winner's parents/guardians will be required to sign and return a statement of eligibility. Names and addresses of the winner and companions may be used for promotional purposes. If another minor is to accompany the winner, the parents/guardians of that minor will be required to sign and return the same forms. 6. Winner and any companion who may be a minor must be accompanied by a legal guardian. 7. Travel and accommodations (based on triple occupancy) are subject to space and departure availability. Reservations, once made, are final and cannot be rescheduled. Certain travel restrictions may apply, including specific blackout dates during peak travel periods. All travel must be completed by December 31, 1992. No substitution of the prize is permitted. The prize is non-transferable. Winner and companions will be responsible for providing their own transportation to and from the airport. For the name of the prize-winner, send a self-addressed, stamped envelope to: "Who Killed Peggy Sue" Contest, Puffin Books Marketing Department, 375 Hudson Street, New York, NY 10014.

WIN A FREE TRIP TO NEW YORK CITY OR LOS ANGELES FOR THREE!

Name _____ Age _____

Address _____

City/State/Zip _____

Phone _____

STORE NAME (where you saw this offer) _____

Store Address _____

City/State/Zip _____

Who Killed Peggy Sue?

(Your answer goes here)

Puffin is pleased to announce the "Who Killed Peggy Sue" contest that could win you three tickets to NYC or LA for a shopping spree.

Just fill out this entry blank and write in who you think killed "Peggy Sue" and the store where you saw this offer. You must be over the age of 12.

Mail this form to:
"Who Killed Peggy Sue" Contest
Puffin Books Marketing Department
375 Hudson Street
New York, NY 10014

Entries must be received no later than November 18th, 1991. Void where prohibited by law. For complete rules see other side.

Winners will receive: Round trip coach airline tickets for three to NYC or LA for a three day/two night stay in a hotel (not including meals or personal expenses, i.e. ground transportation, liquor, laundry, etc.). Winner will also receive $200 per day for shopping spree.
No purchase necessary.